Monsieur Vénus

RACHILDE

Monsieur Vénus
A Materialist Novel

Translated by Melanie Hawthorne
after the 1929 translation by Madeleine Boyd

Introduced and annotated by
Melanie Hawthorne and Liz Constable

The Modern Language Association of America
New York   2004

85 Broad Street, New York, New York 10004
www.mla.org

To order MLA publications, visit www.mla.org/books. For wholesale and
international orders, see www.mla.org/bookstore-orders.

The MLA office is located on the island known as Mannahatta (Manhattan)
in Lenapehoking, the homeland of the Lenape people. The MLA pays
respect to the original stewards of this land and to the diverse and vibrant
Native communities that continue to thrive in New York City.

Cover illustration: photo of French female figure modeled in wax.
Wellcome Library, London

Texts and Translations 15
ISSN 1079-2538

POD 2022 (fifth printing)

Library of Congress Cataloging-in-Publication Data

> Rachilde, 1860–1953.
> [Monsieur Vénus. English]
> Monsieur Vénus : a materialist novel ; translated by Melanie
>   Hawthorne after the 1929 translation by Madeleine Boyd ; intro-
>   duced and annotated by Melanie Hawthorne and Liz Constable.
> p. cm. — (Texts and translations. Translations ; 15)
> Includes bibliographical references and index.
> ISBN-13: 978-0-87352-930-3 (pbk. : alk. paper)
> I. Hawthorne, Melanie. II. Boyd, Madeleine Elise Reynier.
>   III. Constable, Liz. IV. Title. V. Series.
> PQ2643.A323M6213   2004
> 843'.912—dc22   2004019303

TABLE OF CONTENTS

ACKNOWLEDGMENTS

Many people offered thoughtful help and comments that have contributed to the text and translation Rachilde volumes. We would like to acknowledge in particular the work of the MLA Texts and Translations series board. English Showalter did much to improve all aspects of our work and especially the introduction. We are also grateful to the readers of the manuscript, who provided valuable insights and feedback. We owe a great debt to Christian Laucou, who allowed us access to his authoritative but unpublished bibliography of Rachilde's works and who supplied invaluable information about the different editions of *Monsieur Vénus*.

Out thanks to Texas A&M University—especially to its College of Liberal Arts, its Glasscock Center for Humanities Research, its Women's Studies Program, and its Modern and Classical Languages Department—for various research awards that supported the preparation of this work over a number of years. And as always, some things would not be possible without the support of writing groups—you know who you are.

We also thank the University of California, Davis—the Davis Humanities Institute; the Division of Humanities, Arts, and Cultural Studies; and the French and Italian Department—for research support to work on this project. Finally, we thank the UC Davis graduate students for their enthusiasm about the project and for their thoughtful and germane ideas about the project while it was a work in progress: Laura Ceia, Meredith Dutton, Tina Kendall, Kristin Koster, and all the students in Liz Constable's spring 2001 graduate seminar on nineteenth-century Pygmalion narratives.

—*Melanie Hawthorne and Liz Constable*

INTRODUCTION

Rachilde: A Decadent Woman Rewriting
Women in Decadence

A century ago Rachilde's pivotal role among the Parisian intelligentsia was undisputed. Rachilde was a successful, widely read author and a critical conduit and mediator of the aesthetic and intellectual ideas of the time. While her salon brought together aspiring fin de siècle writers and artists, her husband, Alfred Vallette, edited the highly influential literary review *Le Mercure de France*, and she was active in the circles around him.[1] As the only woman writer to contribute to Anatole Baju's journal *Le décadent* (1886–89; "The Decadent"), alongside Paul Verlaine, Arthur Rimbaud, Stéphane Mallarmé, and Paul Adam, she seemed to have secured her place in literary history. But by the time of her death a half century later, in 1953, her work had slipped into obscurity. It has required the recent turn of the twentieth century, along with a scholarly focus on critical comparisons between the two last fins de siècle, to recognize the importance of her work once again.

The writer who became known to the world as Rachilde was born Marguerite Eymery in 1860, the only daughter of a career military officer, Joseph Eymery, and his wife Gabrielle, née Feytaud. Both parents were originally from the Périgord, a region in southwest central France, and it was in a small town just outside the provincial capital, Périgueux, that Marguerite was born. She spent the first decade of her life, however, following her father from town to town around France as his regiment changed garrisons, an experience that is often invoked in her fiction. The Franco-Prussian war of 1870 put an end to this peripatetic existence, and thereafter Marguerite returned to her birthplace to spend her formative years at the family home of Le Cros just outside the village of Château-L'Evêque.

During these years with her family, Marguerite witnessed and experienced the impact of prevailing cultural values about the sex/gender system. First, the very fact that she was a girl met with her parents' disappointment; they did not attempt to hide their desire for a son. Disregard for women was reiterated through her father's verbal and physical abuse of both mother and daughter, as Rachilde frequently recorded in both memoir and fiction. Finally, as an only child with an increasingly unstable mother,[2] Marguerite was often burdened with household responsibilities beyond her years.[3] She reacted by adopting a rebellious persona. Exploiting her parents' interest in spiritualism, she legitimated her authorial voice by channeling other voices. Marguerite's teenage survival strategy, fueled by a strong imagination, showed her to be skillful in inventing ways to elude otherwise constraining and censuring power structures and to give herself "room for maneuver" to become a writer.[4] This skill appears in many of her novels, where female protagonists eschew direct modes of resistance or opposition to stifling power structures in favor of more subtly seductive and yet corrosive (per)versions of the discourses of masculine power (see *La marquise de Sade* [1887] and *La jongleuse* [1900] for examples). This strategy allowed her to appropriate the darkly misogynist topoi of decadence, such as powerful and cruel female figures, and to maintain personal affiliations with male decadent writers, while simultaneously turning around the gendered gaze of decadence to disclose, from the perspective of a woman writer, the ideologies mediating the female figures and forms of decadence.[5]

Marguerite Eymery adopted the name Rachilde from a Swedish nobleman for whom she claimed to act as medium. At first the spirit voice merely served as an alibi for her writing—he dictated stories to her in seances, she asserted. This ploy enabled her to overcome her parents' resistance to her writing. After a few short stories that appeared above the initials M. E. beginning in 1877, the aspiring author published her early work (mostly short stories and serial novels in regional newspapers) under the pseudonym Rachilde, but she gradually assumed this identity permanently and became known as Rachilde for the rest of her life. Her father considered writing an extremely inappropriate activity for a middle-class girl. He also feared that his daughter would perpetuate the legacy of her maternal grandfather, who was a successful journalist and newspaper publisher but in Joseph Eymery's eyes one of those hacks ("des plumitifs") he claimed to despise. But if her father believed that marriage was the only legitimate route to his daughter's emancipation, it is debatable how much he actively opposed her writing. A similar ambivalence, yet differently motivated, marks her mother's attitude toward a daughter-writer. Gabrielle offered her daughter no emotional support or compassion but did provide a legitimate genealogical link to a tradition of writers, one whose details Rachilde embellished in her self-dramatizing autobiographical texts.[6] Indeed, Gabrielle escorted her daughter to Paris while Marguerite/Rachilde was still a minor, arranged for her to meet literary figures, and introduced her to her Paris connections.

In Paris of the 1880s, Rachilde quickly became one of the only women writers in a series of avant-garde literary circles dominated by young rebels reminiscent of their Romantic predecessors of the 1830s, whose exuberance and excesses had prompted Théophile Gautier's satirical account in *Les Jeunes-France* (1833). Grouped in ephemeral clubs with provocative names—the Hydropaths, the Hirsutes, the Zutistes (*zut* means "damn"), the Jemenfoutistes (*je m'en fous* means "I don't give a damn"), and the Incohérents—they explored paths to alternative realities through altered states of consciousness, linguistic experimentation, and erotic transgressions. In rejecting the positivistic and naturalistic tendencies in contemporary aesthetic movements, they searched instead for metaphysical ideals inspired by various forms of mysticism: Baudelairean *correspondances*, occultism, hypnotism, and spiritualism. From these diverse factions emerged the writers associated with decadence and symbolism at the turn of the century. Maurice Barrès's connection to Rachilde deserves special notice (see Finn). Dandified aesthete in the 1880s, then anti-Semitic nationalist in the 1890s, Barrès wrote a trilogy of novels, *Le culte du Moi* (1888–91; "The Cult of the Self"), that valorized cultivation of the self in vigorous dissent to the sociopolitical milieu of democratic France in the newly formed Third Republic. He dubbed Rachilde "Mademoiselle Baudelaire," suggesting that she was a legitimate decadent heir of the Baudelairean aesthetic legacy. In 1889 he wrote a preface to a new (French) edition of her *Monsieur Vénus* that somewhat complicates the praise offered in the nickname Mademoiselle Baudelaire.

In this preface, in lieu of a literary-critical appreciation of Rachilde as a writer, he approaches her text with the diagnostic gaze of a doctor, attributing the bold thematic content of the novel to Rachilde's disorders—nervous exhaustion and perverse instincts—rather than to artistic skills.[7] And yet, while Barrès's preface treats Rachilde's text as the manifestation of a degenerate mind and body (as Max Nordau was to do in general in his influential work *Degeneration* in 1892), this portrait was certainly not unwelcome to the author. As a skillful manipulator of social codes to her own ends and as an indomitable self-promoter of her life as worthy of fiction, Rachilde no doubt considered Barrès's preface an important publicity coup that advanced her career.

Barrès's perspective on Rachilde brings into focus the apparent incongruity of her work within the decadent orientation adopted by other, almost exclusively male, fin de siècle writers. Both Rachilde and Joris-Karl Huysmans borrowed the decadent topos of the Belle Dame sans Merci from the Baudelairean tradition but with different results. *Monsieur Vénus* turns the coldly indifferent, sterile, and cruel figure of Baudelaire's ideal beauty to different ideological ends. Rachilde appropriated Baudelaire's legacy of representing women as split into two sharply contrasting types: on the one hand, idealized woman-beauty as artifice and artifact; on the other hand, organic, embodied woman, monstrously insatiable in her sensual appetites, a degenerate and disease-bearing body.[8] But she rewrote and regendered the male decadent gaze that split woman into a costumed, made-up, bejeweled, inorganic, and inanimate representation of beauty (woman as work of art) and the unadorned person of corporeal appetites. Huysmans also adopts this construction but merely elaborates and develops its duality using the perspective of his male protagonist Des Esseintes in *A rebours* (*Against the Grain*). This novel—published, like *Monsieur Vénus*, in 1884—is widely accepted as the quintessential decadent novel. The divergent fates of the two novels—*A rebours's* fame as a classic of decadence and *Monsieur Vénus's* relative obscurity—tell an important tale.

Rachilde published *Monsieur Vénus* in Brussels in 1884. It was not her first novel (*Monsieur de la Nouveauté* in 1880), but it was her first to win celebrity. Judged to be pornographic, it was banned (in Belgium), and Rachilde was condemned to prison (in Belgium). However, notoriety makes artistic reputations, then as now, and Rachilde made savvy use of the publishing conventions of her day.[9] France had long had a vibrant but clandestine industry in pornographic or "gallant" literature, but it was only toward the end of the nineteenth century that taboo erotic subjects could be openly treated in print. In the 1850s, under the Second Empire, writers such as Flaubert and Baudelaire were prosecuted for obscenity in what are now considered literary masterpieces. Yet just thirty years later, Rachilde could follow in their footsteps without prosecution, at least in France, and claim redeeming artistic merit while exploiting a newly legitimized mass taste for prurient themes. In part, the way had been paved by naturalism, which primed a reading public to accept the idea that literature need not depict only what was noble in humanity; indeed, it had an obligation to confront and represent the basest forms of life, provided that they somehow illuminated human experience. Just as important, with regime change came legal reforms: the more liberal Third Republic was secure enough by the 1880s to allow more freedom of the press (enacted in the reforms named for Jules Ferry). Finally, the popular taste for feuilletons (serial novels published by newspapers) that had created a market for sensational literature was now fed by a growing supply of novels that added an aspiration to artistic merit to the popular writers' sensationalizing of naturalist themes.

In the following years, Rachilde played a skillful double game of "art or life" hide-and-seek with her public. She traded on her reputation as an innocent, reserved, virginal young woman who had produced a shocking book. At the same time, she capitalized on Barrès's portrayal of her as a young writer whose life provided the raw material for her scandalous literary works, a strategy evident in her cross-dressing practices. She followed the success of *Monsieur Vénus* with a series of novels that drew on similar themes of nonconformist, nonreproductive sexual practices, novels that raised questions about the multiple possible relations among the sex category assigned at birth, gender expression, and erotic desires: *A mort* (1886; "To the Death"); *La marquise de Sade* (1887); *Madame Adonis* (1888); *Le mordu* (1889; "Bitten"); *La sanglante ironie* (1891; "Cutting Irony"); *Le démon de l'absurde* (1894; "The Demon of the Absurd," a collection of short stories); *La princesse des ténèbres* (1896; "Princess of Shadows"); *Les hors nature* (1897; "Outlaws of Nature"); *L'heure sexuelle* (1898; "The Sexual Hour"); *La tour d'amour* (1899; "Tower of Love"); *La jongleuse* (1900; *The Juggler*); and *Le meneur de louves* (1905; "Leader of the She Wolves").

During these two decades, Rachilde's circle of literary acquaintances grew to include the most influential literary figures of the age: for example, in the 1880s, she briefly gave up her apartment to shelter the then alcoholic and destitute poet Paul Verlaine. Her Tuesday evening salons (*les mardis*) dated from the early 1880s, before she married the printer and would-be novelist Alfred Vallette in 1889. However, thanks to her husband's founding role in the review *Le Mercure de France*, the circle of writers and artists associated with Rachilde and Vallette greatly increased to include Alfred Jarry, Jean Lorrain, Remy de Gourmont, and Aubrey Beardsley, among others. *Le Mercure de France* made its reputation as publisher of the symbolists, before becoming a successful publishing house that still survives. Rachilde continued to hold her salons until 1930 and enjoyed a privileged role as arbiter of literary taste for several decades. Her influence diminished after World War I, with the emergence of a new generation of writers. Still, she was connected to a group of modernist women writers through her acquaintance with Natalie Barney, whose salon attempted to bridge the gap between the largely expatriate Anglophone modernists such as Djuna Barnes and Gertrude Stein and French writers such as Rachilde and Colette.

Rachilde continued to publish novels in the 1920s and 1930s, but her increasingly conservative views—reflected in her adoption of an explicitly antifeminist public stance, her collaboration with the Italian futurist and protofascist F. T. Marinetti, and her scorn for the Popular Front during the 1930s—left her out of touch with the younger generation. With one important exception: she continued to champion certain forms of sexual freedom. She not only depicted same-sex relationships in her novels, such as *Le prisonnier* (1928; "The Prisoner"), which played a role in the public debates about homosexuality in the 1920s, but she also gathered around her a coterie of young, mostly gay, male protégés, whose careers she supported. Though this move was not entirely disinterested—the ability to dispense such magnanimity was highly flattering to her ego—it testifies to her continued engagement with issues of sexual expression in society.

After Vallette died in 1935, Rachilde gradually withdrew from such active involvement. By the time of the Occupation, she was struggling simply to survive. The Nazis mistook her name for a Jewish one and placed her works on the list of proscribed books, which affected sales—her main source of revenue by this time. Despite her generally conservative views, then, there was little temptation to collaborate (her long-standing hostility to Germans precluded such a thing) and not much energy to resist. She turned increasingly to publishing memoirs, such as *Face à la peur* (1942; "Facing Fear") and *Quand j'étais jeune* (1947; "When I Was Young"), and poetry. She died in 1953.

Monsieur Vénus: Sources, Publication, and Critical Reception

Monsieur Vénus originally appeared as the work of two people: Rachilde and Francis Talman. The identity of Talman remains a mystery. Some people have speculated that he never even existed, but Rachilde claimed she met him while taking fencing lessons and that he agreed to be her coauthor in order to fight any duels that might be provoked by publication of the book. Whether the story is authentic or apocryphal, Talman's contribution to the actual writing was probably minimal, and most subsequent editions of the novel have attributed authorship solely to Rachilde.[10]

Just as she made confusing statements about the authorship of the novel, she offered different accounts of its inspiration at different times and for different audiences. In the preface to her 1886 novel *A mort*, she attributes the idea for *Monsieur Vénus* to amorous transports supposedly triggered by the charms of fellow writer Catulle Mendès. She alleges that her (apparently unrequited) infatuation with him provoked a hysterical, two-month-long paralysis of her legs and that during her convalescence she wrote the novel over a period of two weeks. This account sounds designed to appeal to readers' expectations of further scandalous doings by a hysterical young woman. Barrès's later preface exploited and extended those expectations.

At other times, Rachilde admitted to purely commercial motives for writing *Monsieur Vénus*. On one occasion she supposedly told the following story to a police official, who kept a record of the conversation:

> One day, a Belgian, the friend of a Brussels publisher, said to Rachilde: "You're going to die of starvation. Why not write something 'dirty.' You'll see, it's a good job, you'll be published in Brussels." We looked around together for some filth that people would find new, unforeseen, never before published. In a word, with the Belgian's help, we came up with M. *Vénus*.

When the policeman said that he did not understand the book, he received the following explanation:

> We had some trouble finding something new. Maizeroy, in *Two Friends*, had depicted women's love for each other—[l]esbianism— Bonnetain, in *Charley Has Some Fun*, had depicted m[asturbation] and sodomy. So that way was closed to us. We thought of a woman who would love men and with the means that you can guess, sir—the mechanical arts can copy everything—would b[ugger] them. And there you have M. *Vénus*. (Auriant 62)[11]

This version, though equally suspect, suggests a more conscious desire to write something bordering on the pornographic in order to make money and gain publicity.

A third version comes from a recently rediscovered letter in which Rachilde claimed that the novel had autobiographical origins. In a letter to the symbolist poet Robert de Souza in 1896, Rachilde wrote that the story of *Monsieur Vénus* was her own story. After recounting

how she finally stood up to her father one day when he
was beating her mother, she continues:

> And . . . fearing males, horrified by the intellectual weakness of
> women . . . I fell . . . for a twenty-year-old boy, the secretary of
> our deputy, a perverted peasant who had become a Henri III–
> type minion who wore gold bracelets, and from that day on the
> Monsieur Vénus myth was my own story!

In this account, the genesis of the novel clearly had nothing to do with Catulle Mendès![12]

By the mid-twentieth century *Monsieur Vénus* had
fallen out of print and was known only to a few special-
ists of fin de siècle literature. One symptom of its neglect
is that, although Simone de Beauvoir refers to it in *The
Second Sex*, when cuts were made for the English translation, the reference to Rachilde was deemed expendable
(2: 137). By contrast, Huysmans's *A rebours*, also published in 1884, had attained the status of decadent classic
by the mid-twentieth century. Both novels contain many
of the same decadent topoi: a blurring of distinctions
among the senses through Baudelairean synesthesia; the
confusion between aesthetic taste (art) and culinary taste
(cooking) and between taking in abstract concepts and
eating food; the collapse of apparent opposites such as
disgust and desire, good and bad taste; the relocation of
biblical myths of Edenic creation in decadent hothouses
of artifice; and finally, a rewriting of narratives of creativity itself.

The French publisher Flammarion reissued *Monsieur Vénus* in 1977, but the novel's significance did not
emerge either as fully or as immediately as might have
been expected. Certain factors in the history of femi-

nist criticism may help explain this lukewarm reception. First, Rachilde's fiction frequently portrayed empowered female protagonists whose modes of empowerment over others were aggressive, sadistically seductive, cruel, and violent. Rachilde drew on and reinvented the decadent topos of female figures from both biblical and mythological sources (Circe, Delilah, Judith, the Medusa, Salomé, to name but a few) whose sexual seduction leads men to their literal or symbolic death. Furthermore, her powerful female protagonists (such as the marquise de Sade) are frequently disarmingly unfeminine (as is literally the case for Raoule de Vénérande in *Monsieur Vénus*). Thus Rachilde appears to embrace and reclaim characteristics that would more frequently be identified with abusive enactments of power prerogatives and associated with certain constructions of masculinity or with social class or economic power. During the 1960s and 1970s, the dominant form of feminism in France defined gender in terms of sexual difference and its related concepts: women's difference from men, women's experience, women's culture, femininity, women's writing (*écriture féminine*), and mothering.[13] In a culture structured by masculine ideology, they argued, feminine experience was literally inexpressible if the only language available was masculine. Rachilde's works did not at first seem to provide the sort of material that would lend itself to feminist analysis of this era, since her representation of women clearly went against the grain of giving voice and form to a feminine difference.

For the past two decades, however, cultural critics across the disciplines have been reevaluating the entire sex/gender system, its politics, its role in canon formation, in aesthetics and questions of taste, and in practices of criticism. The issues raised, especially in the areas of literary criticism, cultural studies, art history, gender studies, and queer theory, provide a productive context for reconsidering *Monsieur Vénus*. First, the sexual practices described in the novel do not correspond to any expectations about sexual identity that readers might deduce either from the sex of object-choices or from the specific sexual practices adopted by the protagonists. The novel challenges readers to develop a complex understanding of the axes of gender and sexuality as distinct, although inseparable (see Sedgwick). In this way, it makes visible the cultural processes involved in gendered constructions of sexualities. Second, *Monsieur Vénus* is a powerful rewriting, and inversion, of Ovid's myth of Pygmalion, the misogynist sculptor who, disappointed and disillusioned with mortal women, falls in love with his own creation—the ideal female beauty embodied in his work of art—and who brings his statue to life with the intervention of the goddess Venus (lines 671–765). French writers such as Honoré de Balzac (*Le chef d'œuvre inconnu* [1830]), Prosper Mérimée (*La Vénus d'Ille* [1837]), and Théophile Gautier (*Arria Marcella* [1852]) had used this myth to raise questions about the blurring of aesthetic and erotic experience, about the connections between fantasies and sexual arousal, about the links between looking and desiring, and about what it means to bring an artistic representation to life. Rachilde's rewriting and inversion of the myth makes the artist a woman and the work of art a man.

The aristocratic Raoule de Vénérande (whose name oozes with the contradictory connotations of the venomously venereal and the venerated and venerating Raoule) desires the young ephebe Jacques Silvert, a mediocre landscape painter who lives with his sister, Raoule's flower maker. Rachilde hints at Jacques's femininity through his chosen specialty of watercolor landscape painting, a feminine genre par excellence in the nineteenth century. Jacques starts off as the only artist in the novel, but when Raoule undertakes her seduction of the callow young working-class man, she rapidly stakes out her claim as an artist too. It soon becomes clear that Raoule is a female Pygmalion who fashions from Jacques a corporeal ideal of male beauty after her own desire, "a being in her own image." Her "possession" of Jacques entails a switch of the conventional gendering of mind/body and creator/creation divisions. In two of *Monsieur Vénus*'s key intertexts, the Pygmalion myth and the Baudelairean idealization of the woman of artifice (a work of art), this elevation of mortal being to aesthetic immortality is matched by an accompanying denigration of embodied woman: woman is "natural, and therefore abominable," as Baudelaire put it ("Mon cœur" 893). When Rachilde inverts the genders of creator and creation, she also foregrounds the human price exacted when aesthetic ideals govern life in absolute ways. In the conclusion to Raoule's Pygmalionesque project, Jacques is immortalized as a grotesque blend of wax model and real anatomical parts (hair, teeth, nails). This gruesome artifact throws into relief the sinister subtext of the conventionally gendered aesthetic idealizations of woman:

making permanence out of the transitory and preserving ideal beauty against the ravages of time entails "killing into art" (Beizer 253–54).[14]

Just as significant, as attested by the presence of a plaster replica of the Venus de Milo in Jacques's studio, Rachilde creates *Monsieur Vénus* in the wake of a century of infatuation with representations of Venus in France. This fascination dates back to the unearthing in 1820, by a Greek peasant on the island of Melos, of the fragmented remains of a classical Venus. The statue was subsequently transferred to the Louvre and named the Venus de Milo. In Ovid's story, the goddess Venus animates Pygmalion's statue. During the nineteenth century, Venus came to stand for art itself as a result of the seductive forms, textures, colors, and surfaces combined in her representations. At the same time, her role as goddess of female generation opened onto two quite distinct interpretations of her generative power. On the one hand, Venus represented the goddess of chaste love, mother of Love (that is, the divinity of ideal beauty). On the other hand, as generative Venus, she came to represent the goddess of lust and sensual love, the divinity of courtesans and of *la vie galante*. For nineteenth-century artists and writers, the duality in the image of Venus meant that representations of her could sanction erotic seduction in the form of aesthetic appreciation. Rachilde's *Monsieur Vénus*, in keeping with a decadent fusion of eroticism and aesthetics, makes full use of the fascination with Venus, a trend reflected in continuing debates about gender and prerogatives over creativity (see Shaw 92). For male artists eager to demonstrate the superior transformative power of masculine creativity, Venus, goddess of love and image of female generativity, made a perfect subject for them to master.

In Rachilde's narrative, Venus's nineteenth-century duality as mother of love / divinity of courtesans (a variant of the familiar madonna / whore duality) reappears with a vengeance. When Raoule claims the transformative power of intellection of ideal beauty, Rachilde reverses a gender hierarchy implicit in nineteenth-century aesthetics, one laid out clearly in Charles Blanc's *Grammaire des arts du dessin* (1867; "Grammar of the Art of Drawing"), where the creative and intellectual capacity to recognize and create ideal beauty is presented as an inherently male attribute (see Shaw 100–02). Rachilde's Raoule, a woman who arrogates to herself the masculine right to create her ideal and then embodies it in a male rather than female body, tampers with nineteenth-century gendered hierarchies of aesthetic power and knowledge.

After the republication of *Monsieur Vénus* in 1977, analyses looked primarily at the undermining of gender roles presented in the novel but did not focus either on sexualities or on discourses of art and the ideal (see Hawthorne, "Monsieur Vénus"; Kelly; Felski; Beizer). Dorothy Kelly points out that the novel challenged any sense of stable gender binaries (masculine / feminine), while Rita Felski observes that Rachilde and other modernists connected discourses about perversity to concepts of art as a symbolic refusal of law, thereby making aesthetic and erotic transgression central to the writing of modernity (176). Janet Beizer emphasizes Raoule's reversal of the medical and aesthetic topos of the woman as textual surface:

Rachilde's sustained citation of this topos throughout her novel
is charged with a certain shock value: the reversal of convention,
whereby a male body is appropriated as textual surface by a female
creative force, defamiliarizes the conventional power relationship
and thus puts it into question. (251)

The Different Editions of *Monsieur Vénus*

Another reason why readers and critics did not respond
more enthusiastically to *Monsieur Vénus* in 1977 may be
that they did not realize how truly transgressive and original the novel had been in its first form. The 1977 reprint,
like all other reprints before it and both the previous English translations, reproduced the 1889 Paris edition. All
the early critical work on *Monsieur Vénus* has been based
on this edition or one of its reissues. That text was, however, censored; key passages from the original 1884 Brussels edition were omitted.[15] The present edition restores
the original version and allows today's readers to see
what Rachilde's first readers found in her text.

Monsieur Vénus was first published by Auguste Brancart, a Brussels publisher specializing in erotic titles. This
edition had a four-line preface, signed by the coauthors'
initials ("R. et F. T."), along with the dedication "We
dedicate this book to physical beauty." The cover (often
not preserved in library bindings) bore a quotation from
Catulle Mendès: "To be almost a woman is a good way
to conquer woman."[16] When the novel was immediately judged to be pornographic, the manuscript and all
print copies of it were seized.[17] Brancart responded with a
modified, entirely reset version. This second, extremely
rare edition also bears the date 1884 on the title page.

The cover, however, is clearly marked 1885, though since covers are frequently removed when volumes are bound for libraries, this difference is often not evident. There are, then, two "1884" editions of the novel,[18] easily distinguished even when the cover is missing. To begin with, the title page is slightly different (the publisher's address is given differently). The four-line preface and dedication of the first edition have been replaced by an anonymous short text in the form of a letter (thought to be by Arsène Houssaye). In addition, the penultimate sentence of the novel has been shortened. That this was the only change in the text of the novel to be made in response to the charge of obscenity suggests that the deleted phrase is what most shocked the reading public of 1884. Its significance is discussed below.

In 1889, the first French edition of the novel appeared, and here there were more-substantial revisions. When one compares the first, uncensored edition of 1884 and the censored 1889 edition, there are several areas to consider. To begin with, by 1889, one entire chapter is omitted. Chapter 7, while only three pages in length, represents an important fin de siècle manifesto on the relations between the sexes. It invites the reader to forget so-called natural law, to reject the subordination of one sex to the other, and to contemplate a form of passion with its roots (somewhat nostalgically) in classical antiquity.

Another significant change is found in the heavily rewritten description of Raoule's masturbatory fantasy in the carriage at the beginning of chapter 2, which is reduced from four paragraphs to three in the 1889 edition. That this description was not altered for the 1885 edition suggests that the revisions were primarily stylistic, not motivated by censorship, particularly since the later version seems more overtly erotic than the first. Perhaps the rewriting was done also to eliminate Talman's unwelcome contributions. This fantasy episode is an important echo of the romantic (and some thought pornographic) carriage ride in Flaubert's *Madame Bovary*. In *Monsieur Vénus*, unlike *Madame Bovary*, the heroine needs no amorous partner to share her ride but creates her own solitary pleasure.[19]

Another revision is a short phrase omitted from the novel's epilogue in all editions of the work except the first. That phrase specifies that when Raoule (sometimes disguised) kisses the wax copy of her lover Jacques Silvert's body, a spring hidden inside "the flanks" of the mannequin not only animates the mouth but also spreads the thighs apart. Restoring these words forces the reader to confront the degree of Rachilde's challenge to the sex/gender system and offers some insight into how this novel might have appeared to readers on its initial publication. The phrase accomplishes two things. First, it extends the depiction of Raoule's necrophilia: she is kissing a wax model that stands in for (but finally isn't) a corpse, a model designed to return her kiss. Readers may have found necrophilia and mechanical sexual aids in bad taste, but that may have been Rachilde's intention. Raoule's literal erotic treatment of an idealized dead (male) body challenges the latent necrophilia in the conventions of aesthetic (good) taste, conventions that idealize the woman's dead or dying body.

The phrase also forces the reader to recognize that Raoule is not only kissing the effigy but also performing a more explicitly sexual act. The hidden spring spreads Jacques's legs apart; it does not give him an erection. The suppressed phrase makes it clear that Raoule's relationship with the effigy involves her penetration of him. This restoration sustains Rachilde's claim that *Monsieur Vénus* was about "a woman who would love men and . . . who b[uggers] them" and explicitly challenges the gender hierarchy that the male role is dominant because penetrative. Raoule penetrates yet remains a woman and asserts heterosexuality while reconfiguring body parts to mimic sameness.

The restoration also helps clarify other parts of the novel. For example, Raoule's aunt Ermengarde[20] says that she knows that Raoule is not Jacques's mistress. Indeed, Jacques is Raoule's mistress, and not just because of the social reversal of male aristocrat and kept woman. Raoule does enact a class role inversion just as she enacts gender role inversions, but the restored phrase makes it clear that Jacques is Raoule's mistress because, although biologically a man, he plays the role of the one who is penetrated. The nature of this relationship also explains Jacques's disappointment that Raoule "can't be a man." Furthermore, the phrase allows us to see that Rachilde's redistribution of gender roles and sexual practices goes beyond the category of gender. It is not just that Raoule takes the initiative in sex or is aggressive, behaviors that are sometimes sufficient to make women seem masculinized; rather, she performs a type of sexual act that has no name in the phallogocentric imaginary. This is not the

Hollywood kind of gender bending in which the woman teases the man by acting aggressively in sex but then finally accedes to her prescribed feminine role, in which she dresses like a man but looks all woman once the clothes come off. Raoule's and Jacques's sexual practices exceed any attempt at explanation through appeals to nature, procreation, or the subordination of women—that is, the categories rejected in chapter 7. Moreover, their sexual practices cannot be condensed into categories of sexuality congruent with gender identity as it has traditionally been constructed. Raoule claims simultaneously to be a woman, to be attracted to a man, and to derive sexual satisfaction for herself from the penetration of another. Finally, the use of artificial body parts (Rachilde offers an early model of the cyborg, as Felski has argued) to enact a sexual relationship with a body that is, in the end, no more than a simulacrum takes the sexual encounter into a virtual realm in which any appeal to something grounded in biology becomes impossible. A pinnacle of decadent cerebrality (one of Rachilde's specialties), *Monsieur Vénus* also speaks powerfully to contemporary concerns. The restoration of the original 1884 edition of the novel makes it possible to evaluate her true importance in raising such questions.

Notes

[1]Rachilde's *mardis*, held at her home on rue des Écoles from the 1880s onward, brought together Jean Moréas, Laurent Tailhade, Victor and Paul Margueritte, Jules Renard, and Paul Verlaine, among the best-known participants.

[2]Marguerite's mother heard voices and seems to have had the symptoms of what we would now call paranoid schizophrenia. See Hawthorne, *Rachilde* 185–87.

[3]It is striking that Rachilde created many adolescent protagonists in her fiction. See Dauphiné 63.

[4]Ross Chambers defines "room for maneuver" as the critical space opened up when an oppositional voice avoids strategies of direct opposition. Instead, the opposing voice allies itself with mediation by appropriating the dominant discourse in order to seduce the reader into alternatives to it.

[5]For an analysis of Rachilde's strategy in *La jongleuse*, see Constable.

[6]See Hawthorne (*Rachilde*) for an analysis of Rachilde's strategy of rewriting her life experience as a work of fiction, "treating life as a work of art in true decadent fashion" (15). Rachilde's complex relationships with both parents are discussed at length.

[7]Barrès wrote his preface for the revised, French, 1889 edition of *Monsieur Vénus*. It is published in the 1977 Flammarion edition of the text: 5–21.

[8]See Charles Baudelaire's *Les fleurs du mal*, particularly the poems "Je t'adore à l'égal de la voûte nocturne," "Tu mettrais l'univers entier dans ta ruelle," "Sed non satiata," and "Avec ses vêtements ondoyants et nacrés."

[9]See Hawthorne (*Rachilde*), especially the chapter "1884, May–July: The Politics of Publishing," for extensive discussion of the relation between pornographic and popular publishing in the 1880s.

[10]No other publications under the name Francis Talman are known, and no records exist to suggest that anyone else ever claimed credit for coauthoring. Everything deleted from later editions of *Monsieur Vénus* was recently republished as a literary curiosity for Rachilde enthusiasts under the title *Monsieur Vénus*, by Francis Talman (Paris: Fourneau, 1995). Though no one seriously believes that all and only these passages were by Talman, Rachilde did claim that she later eliminated the passages by him, and the strategy of attributing the deletions to him obviated the need to obtain permission to publish something by Rachilde.

[11]Auriant does not explain how the policeman's notes come to be in Rachilde's possession. For further discussion of the problems surrounding this account, see Hawthorne, *Rachilde,* chapter "1884."

[12]*Soulignac* 196. References to Henri III's minions, or favorites, were often a coded allusion to (male) homosexuality. *Le paysan perverti* is also the name of a novel by Restif de la Bretonne. *Perverti* can mean

"perverted" not only in a sexual sense but also in the more general sense of corruption.

[13]For three key texts that define the priorities of feminist criticism in the 1970s, see Cixous; Kristeva; Irigaray.

[14]On the role of the artist's model in nineteenth-century France, see Lathers.

[15]So far as we have been able to determine, there are three copies of this edition in the United States. One is held by the Library of Congress; the other two are in special collections at Vanderbilt University and the University of Houston. A copy of the rare "1885" edition (see discussion below) can be found in the Widener Library of Harvard University.

[16]For information about these editions, we are especially grateful to Christian Laucou.

[17]The first English translation was published by Covici Friede in 1929 and reprinted in *The Decadent Reader: Fiction, Fantasy, and Perversion from Fin-de-Siècle France*, edited by Asti Hustvedt (New York: Zone, 1998). A second translation, by Liz Heron, was published by Dedalus (UK) in 1992, with an afterword by Madeleine Johnston.

[18]Not to mention numerous *éditions* in the French sense, that is, printings. That there are four known *éditions* of the first edition suggests that Brancart printed 4,000 copies of the novel before it was seized, which is perhaps why so many copies seem to have survived compared with the 1885 edition.

[19]The erotic carriage ride is also a scene reworked with a lesbian theme in Maizeroy's *Deux amies*, the novel Rachilde claimed as one of her (problematic) sources.

[20]Called Elisabeth in later editions.

Works Cited

Auriant. *Souvenirs sur Madame Rachilde*. Reims: A l'Ecart, 1989.

Baudelaire, Charles. *Les fleurs du mal*. Paris: Flammarion, 1991.

———. "Mon cœur mis à nu." *Curiosités esthétiques: L'art romantique et autres œuvres critiques de Baudelaire*. Paris: Classiques Garnier, 1990. 893–95.

Beauvoir, Simone de. *Le deuxième sexe*. 2 vols. Paris: Gallimard, 1949.

Beizer, Janet. *Ventriloquized Bodies: Narratives of Hysteria in Nineteenth-Century France*. Ithaca: Cornell UP, 1994.

Chambers, Ross. *Room for Maneuver: Reading (the) Oppositional (in) Narrative*. Chicago: Chicago UP, 1991.

Cixous, Hélène. "The Laugh of the Medusa." 1975. Trans. Keith Cohen and Paula Cohen. *Signs* 1 (1976): 875–93.

Constable, Liz. "Fin-de-Siècle Yellow Fevers: Women Writers, Decadence, and Discourses of Degeneracy." *L'Esprit Créateur* 37.3 (1997): 25–37.

Dauphiné, Claude. *Rachilde*. Paris: Mercure de France, 1991.

Felski, Rita. *The Gender of Modernity*. Cambridge: Harvard UP, 1995.

Finn, Michael R., ed. *Rachilde-Maurice Barrès: Correspondance inédite, 1885–1914*. Brest: Centre d'Etude des Correspondances et Journaux Intimes des XIXe et XXe Siècles, 2002.

Hawthorne, Melanie. "'Monsieur Vénus': A Critique of Gender Roles." *Nineteenth-Century French Studies* 16.1–2 (1987–88): 162–79.

——— . *Rachilde and French Women's Authorship: From Decadence to Modernism*. Lincoln: U of Nebraska P, 2001.

Irigaray, Luce. *This Sex Which Is Not One*. Trans. Catherine Porter. Ithaca: Cornell UP, 1985.

Kelly, Dorothy. *Fictional Genders: Role and Representation in Nineteenth-Century French Narrative*. Lincoln: U of Nebraska P, 1989.

Kristeva, Julia. "Stabat Mater." 1977. Trans Léon S. Roudiez. *The Kristeva Reader*. Ed. Toril Moi. Oxford: Blackwell, 1986. 160–86.

Lathers, Marie. *Bodies of Art: French Literary Realism and the Artist's Model*. Lincoln: U of Nebraska P, 2001.

Ovid. Book 4. *Metamorphoses*. Vol. 1. Cambridge: Loeb Classical Lib., 1977. 178–235.

Sedgwick, Eve Kosofsky. "Introduction: Axiomatic." *Epistemology of the Closet*. Berkeley: U of California P, 1990. 1–63.

Shaw, Jennifer. "The Figure of Venus: Rhetoric of the Ideal and the Salon of 1863." *Manifestations of Venus: Art and Sexuality*. Ed. Caroline Arscott and Katie Scott. Manchester: Manchester UP, 2000. 90–108.

Soulignac, Christian. "Ecrits de jeunesse de Mademoiselle de Vénérande." *Revue Frontenac* 10–11 (1993–94): 192–97.

SUGGESTIONS FOR FURTHER READING

Anderson, M. Jean. "Writing the Non-conforming Body: Rachilde's *Monsieur Vénus* (1884) and *Madame Adonis* (1888)." *New Zealand Journal of French Studies* 21.1 (2000): 5–17.

Beizer, Janet. *Ventriloquized Bodies: Narratives of Hysteria in Nineteenth-Century France*. Ithaca: Cornell UP, 1994.

Besnard-Coursodon, Micheline. "'Monsieur Vénus,' 'Madame Adonis': Sexe et discours." *Littérature* 54 (1984): 121–27.

Dauphiné, Claude. *Rachilde*. Paris: Mercure de France, 1991.

Felski, Rita. *The Gender of Modernity*. Cambridge: Harvard UP, 1995.

Finn, Michael R., ed. *Rachilde-Maurice Barrès: Correspondance inédite, 1885–1914*. Brest: Centre d'Etude des Correspondances et Journaux Intimes des XIXe et XXe Siècles, 2002.

Frappier-Mazur, Lucienne. "Rachilde: Allégories de la guerre." *Romantisme* 85 (1994): 7–18.

Gordon, Rae Beth. *Ornament, Fantasy, and Desire in Nineteenth-Century French Literature*. Princeton: Princeton UP, 1992.

Hawthorne, Melanie. "'Monsieur Vénus': A Critique of Gender Roles." *Nineteenth-Century French Studies* 16.1–2 (1987–88): 162–79.

———. *Rachilde and French Women's Authorship: From Decadence to Modernism*. Lincoln: U of Nebraska P, 2001.

———. "The Social Construction of Sexuality in Three Novels by Rachilde." *Michigan Romance Studies* 9 (1989): 49–59.

Holmes, Diana. *Rachilde: Decadence, Gender, and the Woman Writer.* Oxford: Berg, 2002.

Kelly, Dorothy. *Fictional Genders: Role and Representation in Nineteenth-Century French Narrative.* Lincoln: U of Nebraska P, 1989.

Lukacher, Maryline. *Maternal Fictions: Stendhal, Sand, Rachilde, and Bataille.* Durham: Duke UP, 1994.

Palacio, Jean de. *Figures et formes de la décadence.* Paris: Séguier, 1994.

———. *Les perversions du merveilleux.* Paris: Séguier, 1993.

Ploye, Catherine. " 'Questions brûlantes': Rachilde, l'affaire Douglas and les mouvements féministes." *Nineteenth-Century French Studies* 22.1–2 (1993–94): 195–207.

Pommarède, Pierre. "Le sol et le sang de Rachilde." *Bulletin de la Société Historique et Archéologique du Périgord* 120 (1993): 785–820.

Rogers, Nathalie Buchet. *Fictions du scandale: Corps féminin et réalisme romanesque au dix-neuvième siècle.* West Lafayette: Purdue UP, 1998.

Weil, Kari. "Purebreds and Amazons: Saying Things with Horses in Late-Nineteenth-Century France." *Differences* 11.1 (1999): 1–37.

Wilson, Sarah. "Monsieur Venus: Michel Journiac and Love." *Manifestations of Venus: Art and Sexuality.* Ed. Caroline Arscott and Katie Scott. Manchester: Manchester UP, 2000. 156–72.

Ziegler, Robert E. "Rachilde and 'l'amour compliqué." *Atlantis* 11.2 (1986): 115–24.

PRINCIPAL WORKS BY RACHILDE

1880. *Monsieur de la Nouveauté*. Paris: Dentu.

1884. *Monsieur Vénus*. Bruxelles: Brancart.

1884. *Histoires bêtes pour amuser les petits enfants d'esprit*. Paris: Brissy.

1885. *Queue de poisson*. Bruxelles: Brancart.

1886. *Nono*. Paris: Monnier.

1886. *A mort*. Paris: Monnier.

1887. *La marquise de Sade*. Paris: Monnier.

1887. *Le tiroir de Mimi-Corail*. Paris: Monnier.

1888. *Madame Adonis*. Paris: Monnier.

1889. *L'homme roux*. Paris: Librairie Illustrée.

1889. *Minette*. Paris: Librairie Française et Internationale.

1889. *Le mordu*. Paris: Genonceaux.

1891. *Théâtre (Madame la Mort, Le vendeur de soleil, La voix du sang)*. Paris: Savine.

1891. *La sanglante ironie*. Paris: Genonceaux.

1893. *L'animale*. Paris: Simonis Empis.

1894. *Le démon de l'absurde*. Paris: Mercure de France.

1896. *La princesse des ténèbres*. Paris: Calmann Lévy.

1897. *Les hors nature*. Paris: Mercure de France.

1898. *L'heure sexuelle*. Paris: Mercure de France.

1899. *La tour d'amour*. Paris: Mercure de France.

1900. *La jongleuse.* Paris: Mercure de France.

1900. *Contes et nouvelles,* suivis du *Théâtre.* Paris: Mercure de France.

1903. *L'imitation de la mort.* Paris: Mercure de France.

1904. *Le dessous.* Paris: Mercure de France.

1905. *Le meneur de louves.* Paris: Mercure de France.

1912. *Son printemps.* Paris: Mercure de France.

1915. *La délivrance.* Paris: Mercure de France.

1917. *La terre qui rit.* Paris: Maison du Livre.

1918. *Dans le puits, ou la vie inférieure, 1915–1917.* Paris: Mercure de France.

1919. *La découverte de l'Amérique.* Genève: Kundig.

1920. *La maison vierge.* Paris: Ferenczi.

1921. *Les Rageac.* Paris: Flammarion.

1921. *La souris japonaise.* Paris: Flammarion.

1922. *Le grand saigneur.* Paris: Flammarion.

1922. *L'hôtel du grand veneur.* Paris: Ferenczi.

1923. *Le parc du mystère.* (Written with Francisco de Homem-Christo.) Paris: Flammarion.

1923. *Le château des deux amants.* Paris: Flammarion.

1924. *Au seuil de l'enfer.* (Written with Francisco de Homem-Christo.) Paris: Flammarion.

1924. *La haine amoureuse.* Paris: Flammarion.

1926. *Le théâtre des bêtes.* Paris: Les Arts et le Livre.

1927. *Refaire l'amour.* Paris: Ferenczi.

1928. *Alfred Jarry; ou, Le surmâle de lettres.* Paris: Grasset.

1928. *Madame de Lydone, assassin.* Paris: Ferenczi.

1928. *Le prisonnier.* (Written with André David.) Paris: Editions de France.

1928. *Pourquoi je ne suis pas féministe.* Paris: Editions de France.

1929. *Portraits d'hommes.* Paris: Mornay.

1929. *La femme aux mains d'ivoire.* Paris: Editions des Portiques.

1929. *Le val sans retour.* (Written with Jean-Joë Lauzach.) Paris: Fayard.

1930. *L'homme aux bras de feu.* Paris: Ferenczi.

1931. *Les voluptés imprévues.* Paris: Ferenczi.

1931. *Notre-Dame des rats.* Paris: Querelle.

1932. *L'amazone rouge.* Paris: Lemerre.

1932. *Jeux d'artifices.* Paris: Ferenczi.

1934. *Mon étrange plaisir.* Paris: Baudinière.

1934. *La femme dieu.* Paris: Ferenczi.

1935. *L'aérophage.* (Written with Jean-Joë Lauzach.) Paris: Les Ecrivains Associés.

1937. *L'autre crime.* Paris: Mercure de France.

1937. *Les accords perdus.* Paris: Editions Corymbes.

1938. *La fille inconnue.* Paris: Imprimerie la Technique de Livre.

1938. *Pour la lumière.* Bruxelles: Edition de la Nouvelle Revue Belgique.

1939. *L'anneau de Saturne.* Paris: Ferenczi.

1942. *Face à la peur.* Paris: Mercure de France.

1943. *Duvet d'ange.* Paris: Messein.

1945. *Survie.* Paris: Messein.

1947. *Quand j'étais jeune.* Paris: Mercure de France.

TRANSLATOR'S NOTE

This translation originated with the intention simply to republish the 1929 version by Madeleine Boyd with minor corrections and changes. Over the course of several years of discussions and criticism, however, it gradually became apparent that the Boyd translation would not give contemporary readers an accurate sense of Rachilde's work and that a new translation was needed. In addition to correcting errors in the 1929 translation and modernizing certain expressions that sound dated to the contemporary ear, it was necessary to look closely at the language of the translation and see the ways it flattened the language of the original by changing sentence structure, "correcting" the French, using the same word in English when different words had been used in the original (and vice versa), and other subtle distortions. The 1929 translation provided a starting point, then, and my debt to it must be acknowledged here, but the present text represents a complete reworking of it, line by line.

The result is a translation that preserves as much as possible the style of the original French, a style that serves as a powerful vehicle of ideological critique. In a manner analogous to Flaubertian irony, Rachilde frequently uses language to expose or make visible the conventionality of cultural clichés and to debunk forms of accepted cultural authority. Where Boyd corrected Rachilde's style by eliminating repetitions, for example, or by joining several short staccato sentences into one more flowing one, the present translation remains closer to the French in order to give Anglophone readers a sense of the specific ways Rachilde works very deftly at the level of the sign.

Nevertheless, there remain nuances of French that are difficult to render completely and yet unobtrusively, and the most notable in this text relate to gender. French has myriad ways of marking gender, from different masculine and feminine forms of the same noun, such as "lover" (*amant/amante*), to the use of adjectives that have no such counterpart in the gender-invariable grammar of English. Gender distinctions have been incorporated as much as possible in the present translation. Also, readers may notice that the connotations of the French *fille* are rendered differently in different places. While literally this term is French for "girl," it can have a number of other cultural connotations, including prostitution. In some contexts, therefore, it has been translated as "whore."

In addition to having more gender-marked terms, French differs from English in allowing two distinct registers of formality in the form of second-person address: the *tu* form, which can connote intimacy, hierarchical status, or even insult (depending on context), and the more formal *vous* form, which connotes respect or distance. Since English allows only the undifferentiated "you," notes have been added to the translation to cue the reader when the register changes in the French.

The subtitle was omitted from most subsequent editions of *Monsieur Vénus*. "Materialist" could be a code word for "atheist" at this time, to signal that the authors subscribed to what some might consider an immoral philosophy that linked them to earlier *libertins*, or free-thinkers.

RACHILDE

Monsieur Vénus

We dedicate this book to physical beauty.
R. and F. T.

PREFACE

We warn our readers that at the very moment they are cutting these first pages, the heroine of our story is perhaps going past their front door.[1]

The use of italics in the English translation conforms to that of the original French text. For their importance, see Beizer 233–36, who argues that "the italics become part of a multi-layered cross-dressing" (233). The works cited in the notes can be found after the text of the English translation.

[1]Most novels in France at this time (and still occasionally today) arrived with the pages uncut; thus books possessed a sort of bibliographic virginity that Rachilde evokes here. It was the privilege and pleasure of the first reader to cut the pages as he or she read the novel for the first time.

Chapter 1

Mlle de Vénérande was groping for a door in the narrow passage that the concierge had pointed out.

This seventh floor was not lit at all, and she began to be afraid at suddenly finding herself in the midst of a hovel of ill repute, when she remembered her cigarette case, which contained the wherewithal to shed some light.[2] By the glow of a match she discovered number 10 and read this sign:

Marie Silvert, flower maker, designer.

Then, as the key was in the door, she entered, but the smell of apples cooking choked her and stopped her short on the threshold.[3] No smell was more odious to her than

---

[2] By making Raoule realize that she can use a match to light the dark hallway, Rachilde introduces early on the information that Raoule is a smoker, still a very risqué behavior for women at this time. Rachilde's contemporary readers, then, would have known from the beginning that Raoule is no ordinary woman.

[3] For the significance of the apples, see Rogers. In addition to noting the more obvious point that the apple "signifies sexual knowledge," Rogers points out the element of cultural transformation implied

that of apples, and so it was with a shiver of disgust that she examined the garret before revealing her presence.

Seated at a table on which a lamp was smoking on a greasy pan, a man, apparently absorbed in very intricate work, sat with his back to the door. Around his body, over his loose smock, ran a spiraling garland of roses, very big roses of fleshy satin with velvety grenadine tracings. They slipped between his legs, threaded their way right up to his shoulders, and came curling around his neck.[4] On his right stood a spray of wallflowers, and on his left a tuft of violets.

---

by the changing state of the apples from raw to cooked (246). This interpretation of a key element of the story of Eden is typical of decadent rewriting of biblical myths of creation in terms of creation as cultural fashioning.

[4]Jacques is depicted as though in mid metamorphosis. His vegetal nature is underscored by his last name. For French readers, *Silvert* evokes both the adjective *vert* ("green") and *sylve* or *sylvain* (English cognate "sylvan"), which comes from the Latin *sylva*, for "forest," an etymology that would have been apparent to those for whom a basic education still included the study of Latin. In this scene, Jacques is positioned to suggest the mythological female figure of Daphne, a nymph who was pursued by Apollo and changed into a bay or laurel tree in order to escape him (a story famously retold by Ovid). This myth is the basis of the use of laurel crowns as a symbol of victory in antiquity. Relying on wordplay, Petrarch could use the laurel (Daphne) to stand for the object of his love, Laura. By extension, Daphne and the laurel come to stand for love objects in general in literature. The subject was also frequently depicted in Western art and painting. The Christian church recuperated this pagan subject by interpreting it as a lesson on the futility of pursuing appearances, a theme developed further in this novel.

On a disorderly pallet in a corner of the room, paper lilies were piled up.

Some branches of defective flowers and some dirty plates, topped by an empty bottle, were strewn between two chairs with broken straw seats. A small cracked stove sent its pipe into the pane of a hinged skylight, and brooded over the apples spread before it, with one red eye.

The man felt the cold that the open door had let in; he pulled up the shade of the lamp and turned around.

"Am I mistaken, Monsieur?" asked the woman visitor, disagreeably surprised. "Marie Silvert, please?"

"You're at the right place, Madame, and for the time being, I'm Marie Silvert."[5]

Raoule could not help smiling; coming from a male-sounding voice, this answer had something grotesque about it, something that the embarrassed pose of the boy, his roses in his hand, did nothing to change.

"You make flowers, you make them like a real flower maker?"

"Of course! I have to. My sister is ill. See, over there in that bed, she's sleeping . . . Poor girl! Yes, very ill. A

---

[5]Jacques's words show the degree to which he assumes a feminine identity. There are numerous other suggestions of, and associations with, femininity in this and subsequent chapters, but here the matter is put quite succinctly.

high fever that makes her fingers shake. She can't supply anything decent . . . Me, I know how to paint, but I said to myself that if I worked in her place I'd make a better living than if I drew animals or copied photographs. Orders are not exactly pouring in," he added by way of conclusion, "but I still manage to get through the month."

He stretched his neck to check on the sleep of the sick woman. Nothing moved under the lilies. He offered the young woman one of the chairs. Raoule drew her seal-skin coat around her and sat down with the greatest repugnance. She was no longer smiling.

"Madame wishes . . . ?"[6] the young man asked, letting go of his garland to close his artist's smock, which was gaping open on his chest.

"I was given," answered Raoule, "your sister's address by someone who recommended her as a real artist. I absolutely must come to some arrangement with her about an evening gown. Can't you wake her up?"

"An evening gown? Oh! Madame, rest assured, no need to wake her. I'll see to that for you . . . Let's

---

[6]Jacques uses the conventional formula of a deferential subordinate such as a shop assistant offering to help a customer, but the broader question of what exactly Raoule desires is central to the novel and anticipates Freud's (unanswered) question: "What do women want?" As Nathalie Rogers puts it: "These words, innocent in the context of a commercial transaction, assume their full transgressive potential in this novel" (243).

see, what do you need? Clusters, garlands, or individual flowers? . . ."

Ill at ease, the young woman wanted to leave. She picked up a rose at random and examined its heart, which the flower maker had moistened with a drop of crystal-clear water.

"You have talent, a lot of talent," she repeated as she pulled at the satin petals . . . That smell of sautéed apples was becoming unbearable to her.

The artist sat down opposite his new client and pulled the lamp between them, to the edge of the table. Thus they could see each other from head to foot. Their eyes met. Raoule, as though blinded, blinked behind her veil.

Marie Silvert's brother was a redhead, with hair of a deep red, almost tawny; he was a little thickset at the hip, with straight legs, slim at the ankles.

His hair grew low on his brow without waves or curls, but it seemed stiff, thick, and resistant to the teeth of the comb. Under his black, well-defined eyebrows, his eyes were strangely dark, although stupid looking.

This man looked at people the way suffering dogs beg, with vaguely glistening eyes. Such animal tears are always atrociously heartrending. His mouth had the firm contour of all healthy mouths, not yet withered by smoking, which saturates them with its virile fumes. At times his teeth showed so very white next to his purple lips that one wondered why those milky drops did not dry up between those firebrands. The dimpled chin of smooth and childlike flesh was adorable. The neck had a little crease, like that of a newborn chubby babe. The broad hands, the sulky voice, and the thickly sown hair were the only clues on him as to his sex.

Raoule was forgetting her order; an extraordinary torpor was taking hold of her, slowing even her words.

But she was feeling better; the jets of hot steam from the apples no longer annoyed her, and the flowers scattered among the dirty plates even seemed to exude a certain poetry.

In a husky voice, she went on:

"The thing is, Monsieur, it's for a fancy dress ball, and I'm in the habit of wearing accessories specially designed for me. I will go as a *water nymph* in a Grévin costume,[7] with a tunic of white cashmere spangled with green beads and rushes; so it needs a background of river

---

[7]Alfred Grévin (1827–92) was a designer and cartoonist who designed, among other things, theatrical costumes. On 5 June 1882, the journalist Arthur Meyer opened a display of wax figures at 10 Boulevard Montmartre and asked the well-known Grévin to create likenesses of the celebrities of the day. Because of Grévin's reputation, the museum was named after him. The Musée Grévin quickly became a popular form of sensationalist entertainment that contributed to the "spectacularization" of the late nineteenth century (see Schwartz).

plants, Nymphaea,[8] Sagittaria, duckweed, water lilies . . .
Do you think you can do that in a week?"

"No problem, Madame, a work of art!" the young man
answered, smiling in his turn. Then, grabbing a pencil, he
tossed out some sketches on a sheet of smooth paper.

"That's it, that's it," Raoule approved, following his
drawing with her eyes. "Very subtle nuances of color,
right? Don't leave out any details . . . Any price you say! . .
. Sagittaria with long arrow-shaped pistils and very pink
Nymphaea, tinged with brown."

She had picked up the pencil to correct certain outlines; when she bent toward the lamp a flash of light
darted from the diamond clasp that closed her coat. Silvert saw it and became respectful.

"The work," he said, "will cost a hundred francs. I will
give you the design for fifty; I am not making much on
it, Madame."

Raoule took three banknotes from her monogrammed
wallet.

---

[8]The name of the common white or yellow water lily indicates its
association with nymphs, semidivine maidens of Greek mythology
inhabiting natural spaces such as rivers and woods. In addition, its
botanical origin—grafted from the eastern lotus—added an exotic
aura: the scent of the flower was thought to be both an aphrodisiac
and a deadly toxin. This connotation gave the nymphaea a special
place in symbolist literature and impressionist painting (see Apter).

"Here," she said simply, "I have every confidence in you."

The young man made such a quick movement, such a burst of joy, that his smock came wide open again. In the hollow of his chest, Raoule saw the same reddish shadow that marked his lips, something that resembled woven gold threads, all tangled up in one another.

Mlle de Vénérande fancied that she might indeed eat one of those apples without too much disgust.

"How old are you?" she questioned without taking her eyes off that clear skin, more velvety than the roses in the garland.

"I am twenty-four, Madame," and clumsily he added, "At your service."

The woman snapped her head away, her eyelids closed and not daring to look again.

"You look as if you were eighteen . . .

"A man who makes flowers—how funny! You are very badly housed with a sick sister in this garret . . . Heavens! . . . The skylight must give you so little light . . . No! No! do not give me back any change—three hundred francs, it's nothing. By the way, my address; write to: Mlle de Vénérande, 74 avenue des Champs-Elysées, Vénérande House. You'll bring them yourself. I am counting on it, you understand?"

Her voice was faltering; her head felt very heavy. Mechanically,[9] Silvert picked up a daisy stem, rolling it between his fingers, and without paying attention used the skilled touch of a trained woman to make the piece of material look just like a blade of grass.

"All right, next Tuesday, Madame. I'll be there, count on me. I promise you a masterpiece . . . You're too generous!"

Raoule rose, a nervous tremor shook her all over. Had she caught a fever among these poor wretches!

That boy remained motionless, openmouthed, sunk in joy, fingering the three blue scraps of paper—three hundred francs! . . . He did not think to pull his smock over his chest, where the lamp lit up its golden gleams.

"I could have sent my dressmaker with my orders," murmured Mlle de Vénérande, as if to answer an inner reproach and to justify it to herself, "but when I saw your samples, I chose to come myself . . . By the way, didn't you tell me you are a painter? Is that yours?"

With a nod of her head she indicated a panel hanging on the wall, between a gray rag and a floppy hat.

"Yes, Madame," said the artist, raising the lamp up to it.

---

[9]A better translation of the French "machinalement" might be "without thinking" or "unconsciously," but the more literal translation has been retained because the references throughout the text to mechanical behavior anticipate the mechanical figure of the automaton at the end of the novel.

With a quick glance, Raoule took in a claustrophobic landscape, where five or six arthritic sheep were grazing furiously on a field of pale green, with so little regard for the laws of perspective that, between them, two appeared to have five legs.

Silvert was naively awaiting some compliment, some encouragement.

"A strange profession," Mlle de Vénérande went on, paying no more attention to the canvas, "because you really ought to be a stone breaker, it would be more natural."[10] He began to laugh stupidly, a little disconcerted at hearing this stranger reproach him for using all possible means to earn his living. Then, just for the sake of having something to say in response:

---

[10]The reference to stone breakers undoubtedly alludes to Gustave Courbet's 1849 painting *The Stone Breakers*, which represents two peasant laborers in a rural setting from Courbet's native province of Franche-Comté. When Courbet's painting was exhibited in the 1850 Salon, in the galleries of the Tuileries, the unromanticized images of laborers marked a significant departure from neoclassical and Romantic painting both in subject matter and in its treatment. The novelist and theorist of realism Champfleury (born Jules Husson) found inspiration for his 1857 work *Réalisme* in Courbet's painting. The reference to Courbet, known primarily for landscape paintings and for elevating working-class people to high art, has obvious relevance to the relationship developing between Raoule and Jacques. Raoule's comment turns Jacques, as a workman, into subject matter for an artist and displaces him from the status of being an artist himself. This allusion marks the first stage of his transformation into a work of art, all the more so since Raoule sees him here as "ce nu" ("this nude"), the artist's model.

"Bah!" he said, "it does not keep me from being a man!"

And his smock, still open, displayed the golden curls on his chest.

A dull pain ran through Mlle de Vénérande's neck. Her nerves were becoming overstimulated by the redolent atmosphere of the garret. A kind of dizziness drew her to this nakedness. She wanted to step back, to tear herself away from the obsession, to flee . . . A mad sensuality seized her by the wrist! . . . Her arm relaxed, and she stroked the workman's chest, as she would have stroked a blond beast, a monster whose existence she still doubted.

"I can see that," she said, with ironic daring.

Jacques started, taken aback. What he had at first taken for a caress now seemed to him merely an insulting touch.

That lady's glove reminded him of his wretched state.

He bit his lip and, trying to affect an insolent attitude, shot back:

"Well, you know, people do have hair all over!"

At that coarse remark, Raoule de Vénérande felt mortified. She turned her head away, and then, among the lilies, there appeared a hideous face, from which two sinister greenish glints were shining: it was Marie Silvert, the sister.

For one moment, without flinching, Raoule kept her eyes riveted to the woman's, and then, haughtily, nodding her head imperceptibly, she lowered her veil and went out slowly. It did not occur to Jacques, stock-still, lamp in hand, to see her out.

"What do you think of that?" he said, rousing himself, when Raoule's carriage, reaching the boulevards, was already on its way to the avenue des Champs-Elysées.

"I think," Marie answered, with a sneer, falling back on her bed, where the brightness of the lilies highlighted the dirt, "I think that if you're not an idiot, we're all set. She's hooked, my pretty boy!"

Chapter 2

When she reached her carriage, Raoule lowered both windows and took a long breath of cold air.

A moment ago, on Silvert's stairs, it had required a supreme effort of willpower not to faint. Her entire, delicately nervous being tensed in an extraordinary spasm, a terrible vibration; then, with the immediacy of a cerebral shock, the reaction came and she felt better. She felt a certain undefined intensity in her being, a bizarre effect quite well rendered by the idea of a spring broken in full deployment, a state in which brain activity seems to increase as the muscles relax.

Raoule recalled Jacques Silvert. The daughter of the Vénérandes, carried away at a gallop by a rapid carriage, returned in thought to the workman of the rue de la

Lune. Nothing remained of the feeling of shame she had felt as she crossed the threshold of the garret. What did the low birth of this man matter for what she wanted to do with him? The envelope, the epidermis, the palpable being, the male sufficed for her dream.

Returning to the precise facts of the matter, her memory supplied nothing that could bring about a pang of conscience. The woman who vibrated within her saw nothing in Silvert but a beautiful instrument of pleasure that she coveted and, in a latent state, that she already held fast in her imagination. With half-closed eyes and a half-open mouth, her head falling on a shoulder raised intermittently by a long calming sigh, she resembled a creature deliciously fatigued by ardent caresses.

Neither beautiful nor pretty in the accepted sense of those words, Raoule was tall, well formed, with a supple neck. She had, like all true girls of good breeding, a delicate figure, slender wrists and ankles, a rather haughty cariage with that undulation which, under a woman's veils, reveals the feline coils. At first sight, her face, with its rather hard expression, did not seduce. Though beautifully drawn, her eyebrows had a marked tendency to meet in the imperious pucker of an uncompromising will. Her thin lips, which faded away at the corners, attenuated in a disagreeable way the pure shape of her mouth. Her hair was brown, twisted up on her neck, and echoed the perfect oval of a face tinted with that Italian bister that pales in the light. Very black with metallic glints under long curled eyelashes, her eyes, two burning coals when lit up by passion, gave at certain moments the impression of two pinpoints of fire . . .

Raoule jumped, suddenly torn away from the depravity of a passionate thought; the carriage had stopped in the courtyard of the Hôtel de Vénérande.

"How late you are, my child," said an old lady, dressed entirely in black, who came down the steps to meet her.

"Do you think so, Aunt? What time is it then?"

"It will soon be eight o'clock. You are not dressed; you must not have dined. Yet M. de Raittolbe is coming to take you to the opera tonight."

"I won't go. I've changed my mind."

"Are you sick?"

"Heavens, no. Upset, that's all. I saw a child fall under an omnibus in the rue de Rivoli! I couldn't eat, I assure you. Omnibus accidents ought not to happen in the street."

Mme Ermengarde made the sign of the cross.[11]

---

[11]In the 1889 edition of *Monsieur Vénus*, this name is changed from Ermengarde to Elisabeth. There are a number of notable Ermengardes in French history (see Larousse's *Grand dictionnaire universel du XIXe siècle* for some examples that Rachilde might have known), but one that might have had special significance for Rachilde is Ermengarde the wife of Aimeri de Narbonne, the renowned paladin

"Oh! I was forgetting . . . Aunt. Come with me. Tell the servants you are not receiving; I have to talk to you about a subject that will please you much more: a charity case. I have come across a charity case . . ."

Together they crossed the immense rooms of the mansion.

There were drawing rooms with such a somber atmosphere that no one ever entered them without constrictions of the heart. The ancient building had two angled wings, flanked by rounded staircases like those at Versailles. The windows, with narrow panes, all extended to the floor, revealing, behind the lightness of dimity and lace, huge wrought-iron balconies ornamented with bizarre arabesques. In front of those balconies, cut across by the entrance gate, was a very Parisian mosaic of plants, those plants of neutral green tints that resist the winter, forming such perfect borders

---

of Charlemagne. Aimeri is a variant spelling of Eymery, Rachilde's family name, and she liked to claim Aimeri of Narbonne as an ancestor (see Hawthorne 84–87). A few centuries later, Ermengarde de Narbonne (1127?–1196?) ruled the city as viscountess. Her grandfather, father, brother, nephew, and grandnephew were all named Aimeri, and, like Rachilde, they liked to claim the Carolingian Aimeri as an ancestor, even though he was probably not a direct relative. Like the character in this novel, Ermengarde de Narbonne remained childless and raised her brother's child. In addition, Ermengarde was celebrated in poetry by the troubadours and is sometimes claimed as an early woman writer; but—in a paradox that Rachilde would surely have savored—none of her actual writings seem to have survived. See Cheyette.

that the keenest eye could not see one blade of grass sticking out higher than another. The gray walls seemed bored with each other, and yet a magician who made those heraldic facades to open to annoy a devout woman would have caused more than one surprise for the retainers wandering in the noble avenue. Thus the niece's bedroom, in the right wing, and the aunt's, in the left, if opened suddenly to the sky, would have made an admirer of pictorial contrasts faint with joy.

Raoule's room was hung with red damask and paneled all around with tropical woods adorned with silk cords. Sets of weapons of all kinds and of all countries, exquisitely proportioned to a feminine wrist, occupied the central panel. The ceiling, rounded in the corners, was painted with old rococo motifs on a blue-green background.

From the center hung a chandelier of Bohemian crystal, a garland of lilies with lancelike leaves and streaked with natural colors. An Athenian couch was placed across the mink carpet that was spread under the chandelier, and the bed, a vessel of carved ebony, bore cushions whose insides and feathers had been infused with an Oriental perfume that filled the whole room with balm.

Some mounted pictures rather free in their subjects were hanging from the molding of the walls. Opposite a worktable strewn with papers and opened letters was an academic drawing of a male nude, with absolutely no shadow around the hips. An easel in a corner and a piano near the table completed this profane interior.

The bedroom of Mme Ermengarde, a canoness of several orders, was entirely of a steel gray that saddened the eye.

Carpetless, the well-waxed floor froze your heels, and the emaciated Christ, hanging near a bed without pillows, was contemplating a foggy painted ceiling like a northern sky.

Mme Ermengarde had been living for about twenty years in the Hôtel de Vénérande in the company of her niece, an orphan since the age of five. Jean de Vénérande, the last scion of his race, had, as he left this world, expressed the wish that the child, born of death, whom he left behind, be brought up by his sister, whose fine qualities he had always greatly esteemed. Ermengarde was then a virgin of forty seasons, full of virtues, smothered in devotions, passing through life as if under the arches of a cloister, lost in perpetual meditation, wearing out the tip of her index finger by repeating those signs of the cross that permit one to dip generously into the treasure of plenary indulgences, and worrying but little—a rare quality in the devout—about the salvation of her neighbors. Her narrative was a simple one. She told it on high holy days, in the unctuous style that inveterate mysticism gives to passive natures. She had had a chaste passion, a passion in God; she had ingenuously loved an unfortunate consumptive, the count de Moréas,[12] a man who was dying every day of the year. Perhaps she had foreseen nuptial felicity and maternal joys, but an unforgettable catastrophe had spoiled everything at the last moment. The count de Moréas went to join his ancestors, armed with the last sacraments of the church. In the extremity of her grief, the fiancée did not scatter her hymeneal roses or rend her white veil; she sought an immortal spouse at the foot of the redemptive cross. Her gentle piety asked for nothing more! . . . The doors of the convent were about to open for her when Jean de Vénérande died. Dame Ermengarde silenced her heart and devoted herself henceforth to the upbringing of Raoule.

At that time a perspicacious tutor would already have discovered in the child the lively seeds of all the passions. As intrepid as she was willful, Raoule never submitted without a cold reasoning that made the tutor's ruler fall on her knuckles all on its own. She brought to the realization of her caprices a frightening tenacity, and charmed

---

[12]In the 1889 edition, this name is changed from Moréas to Moras. Jean Papadiamantopoulos (1856–1910), better known as Jean Moréas, was a poet in Rachilde's literary circles. He published a famous symbolist manifesto in 1886.

her governesses by the lucid explanation she gave of her follies. Her father had been one of those worn-out debauchees who turn red at the work of the marquis de Sade, but for a reason other than modesty.

Her mother, a provincial woman full of energy and with a very robust constitution, had had the most natural and lusty of appetites. She died of a hemorrhage shortly after her lying-in. Perhaps her husband followed her to the tomb, also a victim of an accident he had caused, because one of his old servants used to say that when dying he accused himself of the premature death of his wife.

Dame Ermengarde, canoness, ignorant of the life of material beings, spent her time trying to develop greatly the mystical aspirations in Raoule; she allowed her to reason, spoke to her often of her disdain for soiled humanity, in very choice terms, and made her reach her fifteenth year in absolute solitude.

The moment of initiation could sound in her niece's ear, but Aunt Ermengarde, canoness, would not allow herself to imagine that between the time she kissed her good night and good morning, there was any room for secret ardors that a virgin does not admit.

One day, Raoule, rummaging in the garrets of the mansion, discovered a book; she flipped through it randomly. Her eyes came across an engraving, they looked away, but she took the book with her . . . About that time there was a complete change in the girl. Her expression altered, her words became brief, her eyes darted feverishly, she laughed and cried at the same time. Dame Ermengarde, worried, fearing a serious illness, called in the doctors. Her niece closed her door to them. However, one of them, very elegant in his person, witty and young, was clever enough to get himself admitted by the capricious patient. She begged him to return, and moreover there was no improvement in her condition.

Ermengarde had recourse to the lights of her confessors. The real remedy was advised: "Marry her off," they told her.

Raoule burst into a rage when her aunt broached the subject of matrimony.

That evening, during tea, the young doctor, chatting in the recess of a window to an old friend of the family, said, pointing to Raoule:

"A very special case, sir. A few years more, and that pretty creature whom you cherish too much will, in my opinion, without ever loving them, have known as many men as there are *our fathers* and *aves* on her aunt's rosary. No happy medium! A nun or a monster! God's bosom or that of passion! It would, perhaps, be better to lock her up in a convent, since we put hysterical women in the Salpêtrière![13] She doesn't know vice, yet she invents it!"

That was ten years before the day when our story begins . . . and Raoule was not a nun . . .

During the week following her visit to Silvert, Mlle de Vénérande went out frequently, having no other aim than the realization of a plan she had formed on the journey from the rue de la Lune to her home. She had confided it to her aunt, and her aunt, after a few timid objections, had, as usual, referred the matter to heaven. Raoule described to her in detail the poverty of the *artist*. Who could fail to be moved at the sight of Jacques's hovel? How could he work in there, with his sister nearly disabled? Ermengarde promised to recommend them to the Society of Saint Vincent de Paul and to send some charitable ladies, as titled as they were helpful.

"Let us open wide our purse, Aunt," Raoule cried, carried away by her own audacity. "Let us give alms royally, but let us do it with dignity. Let us put this talented painter (here Raoule smiled) in truly artistic surroundings. Let him earn his living without his having the

---

[13]The Salpêtrière is a hospital in Paris. In the late nineteenth century it was especially famous as the site where Doctor Jean Martin Charcot (1825–93) gave public lectures on female hysteria, using inmates of the hospital. See, for example, Didi-Huberman. Sigmund Freud came to Paris to study with Charcot in the 1880s.

shame of waiting for it from us. Let us ensure his future, right away. Who knows if later he may not pay us back a hundredfold!"

Raoule spoke with warmth.

"My niece," said Aunt Ermengarde to herself, "must have seen a very great, promising disposition in those poor people to make her deign to be so enthusiastic . . . she who is so cold. Here is perhaps a way to bring her back to piety!" For Aunt Ermengarde was not ignorant of the fact that her *nephew*, as she often called Raoule when she saw her taking fencing or painting lessons, was entirely lacking the faith that leads to saintly paths. But the canoness, for her part, was too *worldly*, was too well-bred, had too much *genealogy* in her character, to doubt for a second the physical and moral purity of her descendant. A Vénérande must perforce be a virgin. There were Vénérandes known to have kept this virginal quality through many honeymoons. This kind of nobility, although not hereditary in the family, was entirely binding for the young woman.

"Tomorrow," Raoule finally concluded, "I'll scour Paris to set up a studio. The furniture will be installed at night; there's no need to make people talk about us; the slightest ostentation would be a crime. And Tuesday, when he comes to bring my party costume, everything will be ready . . . Ah! It is on such occasions, Aunt, that our money becomes interesting!"

"I leave up to you, my darling, the celestial benefits of your charities!" Aunt Ermengarde declared. "Spare nothing; as you sow on earth, so shall you reap up there!"

"*Amen!*" Raoule answered, blasé—and smiled like an evil angel at the cleverness of the delighted canoness.

A week later, Mlle de Vénérande, beautiful with an excessively original beauty in her *water-nymph* costume, made a sensational entrance at the ball of the duchess d'Armonville. Flavien X., the fashionable journalist, had a couple of discreet words to say about the strange costume, and, although Raoule had no intimate friends, she discovered some that evening, who begged her to give them the address of her clever flower maker.

Raoule refused.

Chapter 3

In the studio, Jacques Silvert let himself fall back on the couch, bewildered. He looked like a small child surprised by a big storm. So, he was set up in a home of his own, with brushes, paints, carpets, curtains, furniture, velvet, a lot of gilt, a lot of lace . . . His arms hanging at his side, he looked at each thing, wondering if everything was not going to vanish and bring back the darkness of night.

His sister, who still could not believe it, sat down on the suitcase containing their wretched clothes. Hunching her thin back, her hands clasped, she repeated, overcome with immense veneration:

"What a noble creature! What a noble creature!"

She did not forget her eternal cough, like the grinding of a badly greased axle, a theatrical cough with deep chest notes at the end of each attack.

"But we ought to tidy up a little," she added, rising with great decision.

She opened the trunk, took out the picture of the sheep against a clear sky, and went to hang it in a corner. Jacques, moved by an inexplicable tenderness, went over to the picture and kissed it, crying:

"You see, sister, I always thought that my talent would bring us luck. And you used to tell me that it would be better to run after girls than scratch in charcoal on the walls."

Marie guffawed, shrugging her short spine between her shoulders.

"Come on, as if your face didn't count as much as that of your wretched sheep!"

He could not help laughing; his tears dried and he murmured:

"You're crazy! Mlle de Vénérande is an artist, that's all. She takes pity on artists; she is good, she is just! . . . Ah!

Poor working men wouldn't revolt so often if they knew the women of the high and mighty better."

Marie grinned unpleasantly. She reserved her opinion. When she thought of that *high and mighty* woman, all the scenes of vice she had lived through rose like unhealthy fumes to her head; she saw the whole world as flat as her prostitute's bed had been a short while ago after the departure of her last lover.

Philosophizing in a somewhat slow voice that wants to be heard, Jacques was coming and going, scattering the panoplies of armor, which they had not yet had the time to arrange. He stuck all the armchairs against the wall, still not having enough room to walk about and display his new pride of ownership.

The easels of tropical wood were herded into the corner where a very dazzling Venus de Milo stood on a bronze pedestal. He tried to count the busts and brought them to the feet of the goddess, as one piles up pots of mignonette on a grisette's windowsill. At times he uttered little cries of pleasure, caressing the majolica urns and the gleaming foliage of a palm tree that emerged from a hassock in the center of the studio. He even tried the footstools trailing around over the carpeting; he tested them with a thump or threw them at the ceiling.

The window looked out on the most open space of the boulevard Montparnasse, opposite Notre-Dame-des-Champs. Its draperies were of gray satin, bordered with black velvet embroidered in gold. All the draperies echoed these same hues, and the Egyptian portieres, with their strange bright motifs, stood out marvelously against this spring-cloud gray.

After an hour, the studio almost looked like the garret in the rue de la Lune, without the grease spots and the broken chairs; but one sensed that these additions would be there before long. Marie decided that they would put two folding iron beds in the models' dressing room, for the studio had a semicircle with wide curtains, furnished all around with a Japanese screen of pink and blue lacquer. They would dress as best they could, then roll away the two contraptions behind the screen. It even occurred to her to use a huge beaten copper cuspidor as a garbage can. It did not occur to them to raise the portieres, as they supposed that these were as much a part of the decoration as the old trophy armor.

"We'll *wash* those pots," said Marie, full of her subject, "to make some cheap cooking pans. I adore *steam* cooking." She was pointing to the Roman helmets that her brother was trying on from time to time.

"Yes, yes," Jacques answered, planting himself in front of the mirror that reflected back and multiplied all the splendors of his paradise—"do what you like, without tiring yourself. It would be too stupid for you to come down with a fever again here . . . We have other fish to fry. Make yourself at home, pour soup on the sofas, if you like. I'm master, after all, aren't I? You know, I'll have to get to work. The flowers have ruined my fingers. I'll have to get them back in shape quickly. And then . . . the portrait of her aunt, the portrait of her servants, if she insists. I am not ungrateful . . . I think I would willingly bleed to death for that woman. Either there is no God, or else she is one. By the way, our clock is going to strike, watch out!"

The clock, shaped like a lighthouse with a luminous ball on top, struck six, and suddenly the ball caught fire, an opaline fire that made everything visible in a delicious penumbra.

"Incredible," Jacques exclaimed, astonished by this new metamorphosis. "It is time for lights to come on, and the light turns itself on. I'm beginning to think that we're in a play at the Châtelet Theatre."

"There's no vice about it!" Marie Silvert muttered, in response to her own ribald thoughts.

"The clock?" asked Jacques, as naively as a child.

The fact is that the light did not go out, and, as for vice, the clock was spreading plenty of it. The draperies were bathed in a faintly iridescent tint, full of charming mystery. The Chinese monks could be seen lifting their drapery-puffed legs; the terra-cotta nymphs drew themselves up into a kind of floating and intangible vapor, they held out lifelike arms, they let fly human smiles, and the dislocated mannequins made coarse gestures in the direction of the chaste tunic of the imperial Venus.

"Listen, I still have forty sous. I'm going to get a quart of wine and some Italian cheese. Will that do?"

"Yes indeed. I'm dying of hunger!"

Jacques, in his enthusiasm, pushed her toward the door, and soon her footsteps were heard faintly on the staircase.

He returned and threw himself on the huge couch behind the clock. For the last minute his body had been itching with desire for the silk, that thick bushy silk that covered most of the furniture in the studio. He sprawled about, kissing the tassels and the padding, hugging the backs of chairs, rubbing his forehead against the cushions, following with his forefinger their Arabic designs.

Crazed with the madness of a fiancée contemplating her bridal trousseau, even licking the casters, through their multicolored fringes.

He would have forgotten about dinner if a forceful hand had not come into his raging happiness and shaken him thoroughly. He jumped up, trembling, ready to hear the bitter sarcasms of Marie, that eternal malcontent. Then he recognized Mlle de Vénérande. She had entered silently, probably expecting to catch the artist full of admiration at the foot of a statue. She might even have supposed that the brushes would already be primed, the canvas wet, the composition prepared . . . She found a child allowing himself to clown about on new springs. At first it saddened her . . . , then she laughed, and afterward she admitted that it was quite appropriate.

"Well," she said in the clipped tone of a mistress of the house giving an order, "come on, try to be a reasonable man, my poor Silvert. I came to help you; I believe you've no objection."

She examined him.

"Well, what about your working clothes? I hoped that you would know how to make yourself presentable on your own!"

"Mademoiselle, my dear benefactress," he began, following Marie's recommendations, standing up and running his hand through his hair. "This solemn day is the turning point of my existence; I will owe you fame, fortune . . ."

He stopped short, intimidated by Raoule's superb flashing black eyes.

"M. Silvert," she went on, imitating his theatrical tone, "you are a clown, that's what I think . . . You owe me nothing at all . . . But you haven't the slightest common sense, and you'll be condemned, I'm afraid, to overly stiff little sheep on overly sweet meadows. I am a year older than you, and I can sketch a presentable nude in the time it takes you to throw together a peony. I can therefore allow myself some very harsh criticism of your work."

She seized him by the shoulder and made him walk around the studio.

"Is this how you make order out of chaos? Where did you bury your feeling for beauty, then? Answer me . . . I've a good mind to strangle you."

She threw her coat over an armchair and drew herself up, slim, her hair twisted and piled very high, dressed in a black sheath with a long twisting train and trimmed with frogging. Not a single jewel brightened her almost masculine costume with a sparkle this time. Only on the ring finger of her left hand did she wear a signet ring of a cameo mounted on two lions' claws.

When she caught hold of Jacques's hand again, he got scratched. In spite of himself, a feeling of terror ran through him. This creature was the devil.

She jolted things into action in a most cynical way. Scandalized, Jacques pouted! . . . The nymphs reclined on the backs of the Chinese satyrs, the helmets covered the busts, the mirrors leaned back reflecting the ceiling, the hassocks rolled against the frail stands of the easels, and the trophy armor assumed swaggering poses.

"We are lost," thought the flower maker of the rue de la Lune.

"Now come along; you'll have to dress yourself, and I have doubts about whether you'll manage."

Raoule laughed mockingly, thinking that nothing could be done with this fleshy boy.

Then a portiere was pulled aside. Jacques uttered an exclamation.

"Oh! I understand, you have no notion of a bedroom; that's beyond your comprehension."

She lit one of the wax candles that topped off a torchère and led him into a room hung with pale blue. There was a four-poster bed with Venetian draperies in two shades of green through which ribbons of Belgian lace were threaded. Raoule had simply given the decorators what remained from her own summer bedroom. A dressing room with a red marble bath adjoined.

"In you go . . . We'll talk through the curtain."

And indeed they chatted, each behind the dressing-room curtain, he floundering in the water that he found cold, for the bath had been prepared before their arrival, and she laughing at his ineptitude.

"But remember, now, that I'm a boy," she said. "An artist whom my aunt calls her nephew . . . and that I'm treating Jacques Silvert like a childhood friend . . .

"There, are you through? . . . You'll find toilet water above the bath, a comb next to it. Isn't he amusing, this little fellow? God, isn't he funny? . . ."

Jacques was at a loss. After all, high society must be much freer than the society he knew.

And, growing bolder, he let out some rather saucy remarks, asking if she was peeking at him, for that would embarrass him, naturally . . .

He confided in her, telling how his poor father had died caught in some machinery gears, in Lille, his native town, one day when he drank one too many; how his mother threw them out to run off with another man. They set off very young, brother and sister, for Paris . . . His tramp of a sister knew a thing or two already! They had earned their miserable dry bread . . . He said nothing of Marie's debauches, but started mocking himself to drive away a sadness that gripped his heart. They were receiving charity . . . how could he be grateful? Alas, it was quite humiliating, and he was starting to forget Marie's malicious advice as he looked through the shimmering water at the scratches the signet ring had made on him.

Finally there was a noisy splash in the bath.

"I've had enough," he declared, suddenly disturbed by the shame of owing her even his bodily cleanliness.

He looked for a towel and stood glistening, his arms in the air. It seemed to him that someone was rumpling the curtain.

"You know, *Monsieur* de Vénérande," he said in a gruff voice, "even between men that's not proper . . . You're peeking! I wonder whether you'd be pleased to be in my shoes."

And he thought that this woman was absolutely asking to be set on.

"Wouldn't she be sorry," he added in a very bad temper, his senses fully calmed by the freshness of the bath, and he slipped on a bathrobe.

Transfixed, behind the curtain, Mlle de Vénérande could see him without effort. The gentle glow of the candle fell softly on his fair skin, all velvety like a peach. He had his back turned, and he was acting the lead part in a scene by Voltaire, as told in detail by a courtesan called Ruby Lips.[14]

Worthy of the Venus Callipyge,[15] this curve of his back where his spine ended in a voluptuous plane and rose firm and plump in two adorable contours, looked like a Parian marble sphere with the transparency of amber.

---

[14]There is no character in Voltaire called Bouche-Vermeille (Ruby Lips), but in 1725 he wrote a "divertissement" for a party given by the marquis de Livry. In one scene, Voltaire addresses the marquise de Prie, telling the story of a poet who was kissed by a queen while he slept, and encouraging her (the marquise) not to wait until *he* (the poet, Voltaire) falls asleep before rewarding his verses with her ruby lips.

[15]*Callipyge*, from the Greek *Kallipygos*, means "beautiful buttocks." The epithet *callipygean* is applied to certain works depicting the goddess of love, such as the statue in the National Archaeological Museum of Naples.

The thighs, a little less thick than a woman's, were still solidly round enough to disguise their sex. The very high calves seemed to lift the legs just as the buttocks gave prominence to the torso, and this impertinence of an unself-conscious body was all the more intriguing. The heel, very arched, had only one imperceptible point of contact, so rounded was it.

Both elbows of the outstretched arms had two pink dimples. Beneath the armpits and somewhere much lower, a few curly golden hairs stuck out. Jacques Silvert was telling the truth, he had them all over. But he would have been mistaken if, for example, he had sworn that they were the only proof of his virility.

Mlle de Vénérande backed away to the bed; her nervous hands clutched the sheets; she was growling as panthers growl when the supple whip of the tamer has just thrashed them.

"O terrifying poem of human nudity, I understand you at last, I who tremble for the first time in trying to read you with blasé eyes. Man! This is man! Not Socrates and the greatness of his wisdom, not Christ and the majesty of devotion, not Raphael and the rays of genius, but a poor man stripped of his rags and in the skin of a yokel. He is beautiful; I am afraid. He is indifferent; I am aroused. He is despicable; I admire him!

And he stands there, like a child in diapers borrowed for the moment, surrounded by playthings that my caprice will soon take away from him. I'll make him my master, and he will twist my soul beneath his body. I bought him; I belong to him. It is I who am sold. Passion, you give me back my heart! Ah! demon of love, you have made me a prisoner, stealing my chains and leaving me freer than my jailer. I thought to capture him, and he has taken hold of me. I laughed at love at first sight, and now I am smitten . . . And since when does Raoule de Vénérande, whom an orgy leaves cold, feel her brain seething before a man as weak as a girl?"

She repeated the word: "A girl!"

Horrified, she bounded back to the portiere of the dressing room.

"A girl! . . . No; no . . . immediate possession, brutality, stupid intoxication and forgetfulness . . . No, no, don't let my invulnerable heart share in this sacrifice of matter! Let him disgust me before pleasing me! Let him be what others have been, an instrument that I can smash before becoming the echo of its vibrations!"

She pulled aside the drapery with an imperious gesture. Jacques Silvert had hardly finished sponging himself dry.

"Child, do you know that you are marvelous?" she said to him with cynical frankness.[16]

The young man cried out and picked up his dressing gown. Then, sorrowfully, quite pale with shame, he let it fall passively, because, poor boy, he understood. Was not his sister cackling from a corner: "Go on, idiot, you who thought you were an artist. Go on, contraband plaything, go on, love toy, do your job."

This woman had pulled him away from his garlands of artificial flowers, the way one rips from a real flower the rare insect that one wants to place like a jewel on a decoration.

"Go on, you spineless creature! Girls from the nobility don't have pals. Depraved women know how to choose! . . ." It seemed to him he was hearing all those insults humming through his reddening ear, and his virginal blondness took on the same rosiness, while his two nipples, aroused by the water, stood out like two Bengal rosebuds.

"Antinous[17] must have been one of your ancestors, I think?" Raoule muttered, throwing her arms around his neck and obliged by her height to lean on his shoulders.

---

[16]This is the first time that Raoule addresses Jacques using the familiar *tu* ("you"). At first it might seem appropriate, since she is addressing him as a child, but she continues to use this form for the remainder of this chapter.

[17]Antinous was a Bithynian slave who became the favorite of the Roman emperor Hadrian. Antinous is thus both a paragon of male beauty and a coded reference in some texts to male homosexuality.

"I never met him!" answered the conqueror, humiliated, bowing his head.

Ah! All the wood he had chopped for the wealthy, all the bread crusts he had picked up in the gutter, the poverty bravely borne, in spite of the perfidious advice of his sister, the prostitute! . . . His part as a worker artfully played, the ridiculous little tools tiring fate with their perseverance, where had it all gone? And how much better was that! Respectability was not his strong point, but one could have been nice about it until the end, leaving him his illusions and time to make a fortune to return the favor some day . . .

"Will you love me, Jacques?" asked Raoule, shivering at the contact of his naked body, frozen to the marrow by the horror of his fall.

Jacques knelt on the train of her gown. His teeth were chattering. Then he burst into tears.

Jacques was the son of a drunkard and a whore. All he could honorably do was cry.

Mlle de Vénérande raised his head; she saw those burning tears roll down, and felt them falling one by one on her heart, the heart she had tried to deny. The room suddenly appeared to be suffused with dawn; it seemed to her she was breathing an exquisite perfume, released suddenly into the enchanted atmosphere. Her whole being dilated, immense, encompassing at the same time all earthly sensations, all heavenly aspirations, and Raoule, vanquished, proud, cried:

"Stand up, Jacques, stand up! I love you!"

She pulled him off her dress, and ran to the door of the studio repeating:

"I love him! I love him!"

She turned around again:

"Jacques, you are master here . . . I'm leaving. Good-bye forever. You'll never see me again! Your tears have purified me and my love is worth your forgiveness."

She ran away, crazed by an atrocious joy, more voluptuous than the pleasures of the flesh, more aching than unappeased desire, but more complete than orgasm, crazed by that joy called the emotion of a first love.

"Well," said Marie Silvert quietly after she had left, "it seems the fish is biting . . . Everything will go like clockwork, I'll be damned!"

Chapter 4

Marie had the letter in her pocket; she was firmly convinced now that the madwoman would resist no longer, that she would return to them wiser, more protective, in short more *loaded*, in her working-class parlance, and that new splendors were sure to rain down. Damn! Millions would come and stick to the boy like jelly on a cold beef stew; he would wear his Sunday best every day; she would trail around her smelly kitchens in moiré dresses. He would be called Monsieur, and she would be Madame!

The letter had few lines, but it explained a host of things quite clearly:

"Come," the prostitute had written with spelling mistakes and blue ink.[18] "Come! dear wife of your little Jacques . . . I languish without you . . . we have spent the three hundred francs and I've had to send Marie to sell a pot with a snake on it. It's sad to see oneself abandoned so quickly after tasting heaven . . . You understand, don't you? I think I'm going to fall ill. As for my sister, she's still coughing.

"Your unquenched lover,

" Jacques."

When she had finished this masterpiece, Marie, in spite of her brother's distressed countenance, set off for the avenue des Champs-Elysées. That idiot would never know how to take his part seriously. Fortunately she was placing her experience of the human body at his disposal, and she knew, on important occasions, how to *touch* what lies beneath the breast of a lover, male or female.

It was raining that day, a March rain, slow and penetrating; the mud was deep in all the paths of the avenue.

---

[18]Marie has Jacques address Raoule with the *tu* form of the verb.

Marie had tried to economize by not taking a carriage, so she was soon splattered from head to foot.

When she reached the mansion, that large somber-looking building, she wondered if she would be thrown out as soon as she entered the hall. At the top of the front steps she found a big porter and a small dog. The first took the letter; the second growled.

"Do you want to see Mademoiselle or Madame?"

"Mademoiselle."

"Hey! Pierrot, there's a woman here who wants to sweep the stairs, as it were," the porter shouted to a microscopic page passing through the hall.

It was quite funny, really; but the page, part of Mademoiselle's personal staff, grimaced like a man who believes anything possible, even on a rainy day.

"All right, I'll see. Wait here."

He pointed to a bench. Marie did not sit down, and said coarsely:

"I don't hang about in antechambers. Do you take me for a retired charwoman, monkey face?"

Dumbfounded, the page turned on his heel, and like a well-trained servant, muttered:

"Someone with influence!" For under the Republic, clothes mean less and less all the time.

Mademoiselle was in a boudoir adjoining her bedroom. When Mme Ermengarde went out, Raoule received visitors of both sexes in her own apartment. This boudoir opened onto a conservatory, which she had turned into her study. When the page burst in, a man was pacing rapidly back and forth in the conservatory, while Mlle de Vénérande was stretched out on a Creole love seat rocking and laughing out loud.

"You're condemning me to hell, Raoule," repeated the man who was still young and had a dark Slavic face, though one enlivened by a Parisian vivacity.[19] "Yes, you're condemning me to hell, supposing I weren't already headed there . . . Laughter is not an answer . . . I tell you a woman can't live without love, and you know that by love I mean the union of souls through the union of bodies. I'm frank. I never wrap up a plain statement in pretty trimmings, the way people disguise bitter medicine with jam . . . I'm speaking to you bluntly, as a hussar should, and when I see the ditch, I don't waste my time picking petals off daisies. No, I use the spurs and let you have it, Raoule de Vénérande, *my dear comrade!* All right, don't get married! But at least take a lover: it's necessary for your health."

---

[19]Raittolbe uses the polite, respectful *vous* form of address, and Raoule replies in the same way. *Vous* signals a certain equality and mutual respect that is maintained in their relationship; it stands in marked contrast to the inequalities (suggested by the shifts between *tu* and *vous*) that mark Raoule's relationship with Jacques.

"Bravo! M. de Raittolbe! I'll even bet that my health won't really flourish unless my lover is an officer in the hussars, dark, with frank speech, impertinent eyes, and a commanding voice, right?"

"Indeed I admit it, I will even go further . . . I propose the same hussar as a husband . . . Take your pick! Seniority or exceptional service! There are five of us who have been courting you madly for the last three years. Prince Otto, the music fanatic, has gone insane apparently and placed your full-length portrait in a mortuary chapel, where yellow wax candles burn around the magnificent bed of rest . . . and there he sighs from dawn to dusk. Flavien, the journalist, runs a trembling hand through his hair whenever your name is mentioned. Hector de Servage, after the plain dismissal given him by your aunt, has gone to Norway to cool off. Your fencing master almost stuck one of his best swords between his ribs. So, your humble servant being the only one left . . . having the honor to hold your stirrup for your promenades in the Bois,[20] I imagine you must look at him with the least disfavor, and he urges his candidacy. Raoule, would you

---

[20]The Bois de Boulogne (Boulogne Wood) is a famous park on the (then) western edge of Paris. In the late nineteenth century one could ride horses there. A ride in an open carriage in the park during the afternoon was also an important social ritual for the upper class (and those who aspired to it).

like to shelter our friendship in a conjugal alcove? It will be warmer . . ."

Raoule had risen and was going toward M. de Raittolbe when the page entered.

"Mademoiselle, here is an urgent letter."

She turned around.

"Give it to me."

"You'll excuse me?" she added, turning to the hussar, who was breaking a Japanese plant into tiny pieces in an effort to vent his rage. He turned his back on her, too furious to answer. It was the thousandth time that this conversation had broken off at the most interesting moment.

M. de Raittolbe, impatient, sullenly lit a cigar and fumigated a whole border of azaleas, swearing to himself that he would never come back to this hysterical woman, for, in his opinion, anyone who did not follow the ordinary rules must be hysterical.

Raoule grew pale as she read the letter.

"Good God!" she muttered. "He wants money; I have fallen into the mire!

"Have this poor creature sent up," she went on lightly. "I insist on giving her what she wants at once."[21]

---

[21]The original French leaves it ambiguous as to whether Raoule is expecting to see Jacques or Marie. The subject pronoun *elle* in "ce qu'elle désire" may refer back to "créature," a noun that is grammatically feminine regardless of referent.

"And on refusing me the explanation I want?" the officer grumbled, beside himself with anger.

Raoule quietly closed the conservatory door on him, returned to her boudoir, and sat down as pale as a corpse. She bent her head and dug her long nails into the letter covered with blue ink.

"Money! Oh! no, I won't give in! I'll send him what he wants, instead of going to kill him! . . . Is it his fault? Can a man of the lower classes, just because he has beauty, not also be abject? Well, I'm glad that this cup of bitterness has been offered to me. I won't refuse it . . . on the contrary, I'll drink new life from it."

Marie Silvert's racking cough made her lift her head. Raoule stood up, suddenly threatening and more haughty than a goddess speaking from the empyrean.

"How much?" she said, spreading out the immense train of her velvet dress behind her.

Marie finished her fit of coughing . . . she had not expected that question so soon . . . Damn! things were going badly . . . They ought to have begun more gently, with talk of feelings, tender questions . . . A caprice must be allowed to simmer like a stew, with the pepper added at the last minute.

"Poor Jacques is lonely, you know?" she declared with a smile full of sordid implications.

"How much?" repeated Raoule, seized by a blind anger and looking around for a knife.

"Don't get angry, Mademoiselle. In his letter money is just a manner of speaking; really the child just wants to see you . . . He's an unreasonable baby, an oversensitive crybaby! He thought that your crush was already over, and it was time to make himself scarce, there was nothing to be done. If he doesn't see you again, I'm really afraid he'll do away with himself. This morning, as he looked at his glass, he told me it would soon serve him poison. Poor kitten! It's enough to break your heart! At his age! And so fair, so white! Well, you know how he is? So I put on my Sunday dress . . . Don't leave your brother in agony, I told myself. And here I am! As for money, we are poor but proud. We can talk about that later! . . ."

She wiped her foot on the boudoir carpet, feeling secretly pleased at soiling the *high and mighty* a little, and shook the faded umbrella from which she had refused to be parted.

Raoule went straight to the cabinet opposite her; with the back of her hand she thrust the woman aside, as one throws aside an old rag when it is about to slap you in the face.

"I have a thousand francs, here . . . I'll send you another thousand tonight . . . but leave at once . . . I don't know your brother . . . I don't know where he lives . . . I don't know your name. Take it and go!"

She put the notes down on an armchair, motioned to Marie to pick them up. Then she rang the bell.

"Jeanne," she said to her chambermaid, "show Madame out."

"Well!" the flower maker grumbled, very much surprised.

She was led away, almost at arm's length, by Jeanne. A shove from the porter pushed her into the avenue, while the small dog, following her down the steps, added a few shrill howls.

"Are you lonely, baron?" Raoule asked smilingly as she entered the conservatory.

"Mademoiselle," Raittolbe answered, acutely impatient, "you are a pleasant monster, but studying wild animals really only has charm in Algeria . . . So I'll say good-bye to you tonight; tomorrow I'll set sail for Constantine. I don't care who holds your stirrup for you. Personally, I can't take it anymore."

"Ah ha! I seem to remember, however, that only a short while ago you offered me your name! . . ."

Raittolbe clenched his fists.

"To think that I resigned my commission to hunt tigers!" he went on, not even listening to her.

". . . that you asked me in fact to marry you! . . ."

"... when I can hunt a tiger in the grounds of the Vénérandes, a tiger dressed up as an amazon ..."[22]

[22]The amazon figure was at the nexus of a number of related concerns about woman's place at the end of the nineteenth century in France. The Amazons were a tribe of female warriors on horseback, according to ancient Greek historians such as Herodotus, and thus they came to be associated with all forms of female militancy, but *amazon* later acquired a number of other connotations. At the fin de siècle, *amazon* could simply designate a female horse rider (riding amazon style initially meant riding sidesaddle), but the female equestrian in the late nineteenth century was also associated with (illicit) creativity and sexuality. Horse training for women became synonymous with the breaking of men, for example. Riding astride a horse was considered unseemly for women, because it entailed the inappropriate spreading of legs. This anxiety expressed itself in concerns about how riding might offer inappropriate genital stimulation (or harm reproductive organs), an anxiety that applied also to the female bicycle rider. The female cyclist was a stereotype for the (sexually) liberated woman of the turn of the century (Rachilde used it in her depiction of Missy in *La jongleuse*). One particular model of bicycle then was called the Dahomien, a reference to the Amazons of Dahomey (the Greek myth was revived in accounts of conflicts between French colonial forces in Dahomey and indigenous resistance). The need for freedom of movement in the legs necessary for riding (both horses and bicycles) also led to the broader challenge to social and legal rules about the wearing of trousers (a debate familiar in the United States through the advocacy of bloomers for female cyclists). In France, one of the first official relaxations of legislation against female cross-dressing came in the form of an exemption for women who were accompanied by a horse or a bicycle (certain medical and work-related exemptions were already allowed). That such activities (the riding and the clothing associated with it) were viewed as a challenge to gender boundaries is reflected in the description of the new woman as a *garçonne* (morphologically a female boy). As an extension of the perception that the amazon violates gender expectations, *amazon* can also serve as a coded reference to female homosexuality. For more on the female equestrian and her connotations, see Weil.

". . . without asking my aunt or observing the rules of etiquette, sir!"

". . . I'm making myself ridiculous, Mademoiselle!"

"Yes, I think you are," Raoule added philosophically.

The baron de Raittolbe was taken aback. They looked at each other a moment, then burst out laughing.

Encouraged by this, the young man seized the young woman's hands, and they went and sat on a couch in the conservatory, a magnolia behind them.

"Listen, sincere love can never be ridiculous. Raoule, I really love you."

He bent down. His somewhat mocking eyes filled with tears that were only due to nervous facial exertion, and not to the tenderness of which he wished to speak to her, then he kissed her fingers one by one, stopping to look up at her between each caress.

"Raoule . . . I gave you my heart . . . I will not leave without taking it back, and since I've put it next to yours, I hope that you'll mix them up . . . two boys' hearts, two hussars' hearts must both be much the same color red . . . Give me yours . . . keep mine . . . In a month we'll be hunting real lions together in real Africa."

"I accept!" Raoule answered, and her dark eyes, which did not know how to cry, looked suddenly mournful.

"What, you accept?" Raittolbe said, his heart tightening.

The young woman, with supreme dignity, thrust away his outstretched hands.

"I accept you as a lover, my dear. You won't be the first, and I am a *gentleman*! . . ."

"I knew it," Raittolbe replied gently, "and now I think I adore you!"

That evening the young officer dined with the Vénérandes. Toward Aunt Ermengarde he was the most courteous of knights. He made a speech about the devotion that blinds woman to human failings and raises her above this impure earth. Aunt Ermengarde admitted that the hussars were good boys. As he took his leave, Raittolbe whispered a word in Raoule's ear:

"I'll wait . . ."

"Tomorrow," she murmured, "at the Hôtel Continental. My brown carriage will come in by the left entrance about ten in the morning."

"At your service."

And the man about town went away at peace.

The next day the brown carriage was ordered about ten, and Raoule threw herself in with feverish gaiety. Indeed, it would be so, she had promised herself, and since he was, in the end, better than the others, perhaps he would amuse her more. A slip of the senses is not the flowering of a soul, and the beauty of one human body alone is not capable of inspiring an eternity of mad attachment to it.

She sang as she buttoned her gloves. The window of the carriage reflected her image; her corsage flowing with lace suited her; she felt like *a woman* right through to her pleasure.

"Does Mademoiselle wish to go in?" said the coachman, leaning through the window at the end of a fast run.

"No, just stop, and when I get out, drive in at the left and wait for me till this evening! . . ."

Raoule's voice had grown shrill. She got out, saw a standing cab, and hurried over.

"Notre-Dame-des-Champs, boulevard Montparnasse!" she said, as the other carriage, empty, headed toward the left entrance, as she had ordered.

During the entire drive she had not thought about it, but once confronted with the sacrifice, her body, no longer in control of itself, revolted. Raoule had given in without demur.

The studio in the boulevard Montparnasse seemed lugubrious when she arrived, but at the back she saw the bedroom, as blue as a corner of the sky. Marie Silvert left as soon as Raoule crossed the threshold.

"Well," she said, "we'll settle our little business after lunch. It will be pretty heated, I assure you, you slut!"

To isolate herself, Mlle de Vénérande undid the heavy portieres.

"Jacques! . . . ," she called sharply.

He hid his face in his pillow, unwilling to believe this final infamy.

"I didn't write the letter!" he shouted. "I assure you, I wouldn't have dared.[23] Besides, I want to leave, I'm sick. Making me ill forces me to stay in bed . . . Marie is capable of anything, I know her! You! . . . I can't stand you! . . ."

His energy exhausted, he slid back under the covers, curling up like a beaten animal.

"Is that so?" asked Raoule, jolted by a delicious shiver.

"Yes, that's so!" He stuck out his tousled head, while his lovely fair complexion took on a pinkish tint.

"Then why did you allow the letter to be sent?"

"I didn't know, did I! Marie assured me I had a fever, *her fever*. She gave me some drug, and I was delirious every night. She said it was quinine. I would have stopped her, but I wasn't strong enough. Ah! You can take it all back, your wretched studio! Oh, God! . . ."

Out of breath, he tried to sit up, which made Raoule notice a strange thing: he was wearing a woman's nightgown, an embroidered nightgown.

"And is she the one who decks you out like this?" Raoule said, touching the embroidery around his neck.

---

[23]Jacques uses the *vous* form to address Raoule. Not only would he "not have dared" to write to Raoule, but he does not presume to address her with the *tu* form.

"Do you think I own any underwear? My tatty old rags have all been thrown away a long time ago. I was cold, she stuck this on me . . . How am I supposed to know it's a woman's nightgown! . . ."

"Well, it is, Jacques!"

They looked at each other for a moment, wondering whether or not to laugh.

Marie shouted from the back of the studio:

"I'll lay the table for two, right? . . ."

Then, willing to agree to anything if it would appease his shame, which was beginning to intoxicate her, Raoule de Vénérande bolted the door, while Jacques started to laugh heartily. Then she came back, haltingly, toward the bed. He had a sweet, childish, and charmingly silly laugh, a provocative laugh full of grace, one that gave you nasty thrills. She did not try to analyze the attraction behind this silliness; she let herself sink into it, as a drowning man, his struggles over, yields to the wave and abandons himself to the current forever. She pulled aside the blue curtains to see the young man's face.

"Are you sick?" she asked mechanically.

"Not since you came," he answered in a triumphant voice.

"Do you want to do something for me, Jacques?"

"Anything, Mademoiselle!"

"Then shut up. I didn't come here to listen to you."

He fell silent, somewhat vexed, saying to himself that doubtless his compliment had not sounded very new to this sophisticate. Real high-society women are rather intimidating in intimate relationships, and he realized that he had made a bad start; he was still feeling his way too much, he realized.

"I'm going to sleep!" he declared suddenly, pulling the sheet up to his nose.

"That's it! Go to sleep," Mlle de Vénérande murmured. On tiptoe she pulled the blinds, then lit a nightlight whose frosted glass left a soft haze in the atmosphere.

From time to time, Jacques raised his eyelashes, and the discreet movements of this slender woman, dressed all in black, caused him a terrible embarrassment.

Finally, she came up to him holding a small tortoiseshell box.

"I have brought you," she said with a motherly smile, "a remedy that is not at all like your sister's quinine. It'll help put you to sleep! . . ."

She put her arm around his head and a silver spoon in reach of his mouth.

"Be good! . . . ," she said, looking solemnly into his eyes.

"I don't want any!" he declared in an angry tone. He remembered now a nasty, cheap book that he had bought on the quays of the Seine in a moment of recklessness, entitled *The Exploits of Madame Brinvilliers*,[24] and the loves of grand ladies always made him think of poisoning. His weakened brain suddenly recalled the image of someone in a velvet cloak criminally attacking an undressed man. He saw the man pushing the cup away with a twisted gesture. Raoule surely wanted to get rid of him. There are creatures who stop at nothing when they think they have compromised themselves! So Jacques clenched his fist in front, ready to crush her at the first attack. Raoule's only response was to nibble the contents of the spoon with her teeth.

"I'm not a baby!" he said, disoriented. "There's no need to chew things for me." And without batting an eye he swallowed the greenish remedy with the taste of honey.[25] Raoule sat on the edge of the bed, holding both his hands and smiling, both happy and sad at the same time.

---

[24]The marquise de Brinvilliers was executed in 1676 after a trial that led to her conviction for having poisoned her father and two brothers. She was the subject of a number of works in the nineteenth century. Edmé Pirot's *La marquise de Brinvilliers, récit de ses derniers moments*, for example, appeared in 1883.

[25]The references to green paste or jam were no doubt familiar to Rachilde's readers as allusions to hashish (sometimes mixed with opium). Baudelaire, for example, repeatedly refers to it as "confiture verte" ("green jam") in his essays on wine and hashish, such as "Du vin et du haschisch" (1851) and "Les paradis artificiels" (1860). Rachilde's description of Jacques's hallucinations may be compared with Baudelaire's account of the effects of a spoonful of hashish taken in a cup of coffee, in chapter 4 of "Du vin et du haschisch," for example.

"My love," she whispered, so quietly that she sounded to Jacques as if she were speaking from the bottom of an abyss, "now we'll belong to each other in a strange country where you've never been.

"It is the country of madmen, but not the country of brutes . . . I've come to take away your vulgar senses and give you others more subtle, more refined. You'll see with my eyes, taste with my lips. In this country, dreams are the only life. You'll dream, and then you'll understand, when I appear in your dream, everything you don't understand when I'm speaking to you now!

"Go! I won't hold you back any longer, and I'll add my heart to your pleasures! . . ."

Jacques, his head thrown back, tried to hold on to her hands. He felt himself sliding little by little into a bath of feathers. The curtains dissolved, and the multiplying mirrors in the room reflected a thousand times the silhouette of a woman in black, immense, gliding like a genie turned into a puff of smoke and thrown from the highest skies. He tensed all his muscles, stiffened all his limbs, trying in spite of himself to return to the earthly envelope that was being taken away from him, but falling in deeper and deeper. The bed had disappeared, and so had his body. He was spinning in the blue, turning into a creature like the soaring genie. At first he thought he was falling, but on the contrary he found himself floating above this world. Inexplicably, he had the proud feeling of Satan, who, though fallen from Paradise, still looks down on the earth and has, at one and the same time, his forehead under God's heel and his own heel on the forehead of man!

He seemed to live like this for centuries, with the woman in black and himself resplendent in a luminous nudity.

In his ear he could vaguely hear the songs of a strange sexless love that produced every kind of pleasure. He loved with an awful power and with the ardor of a burning sun. He was loved with a terrifying abandon and with such exquisite knowledge that joy was rekindled each time it seemed about to disappear.

Infinite space opened before them, always blue, always dazzling . . . and down below, in the distance, a sort of outstretched animal seemed to be watching them gravely . . .

Jacques Silvert never knew how, during that moment of almost divine happiness, he managed to get up. As he came to, he found that he was standing, his heel resting nervously on the head of the big bear that served as a bedside rug. His eyes looked wildly into a Venetian mirror, and the room was very quiet. Behind the portiere a voice asked:

"Are you ready for dinner, Mademoiselle?"

Jacques could have sworn that it was only a minute ago that someone had asked, "Are you ready for lunch? . . ."

He dressed hastily, moistened his temples with a sponge dipped in astringent, and stammered:

"Where is she? I don't want her to leave!"

"Here I am, Jacques!" a voice answered. "I didn't leave you, since you were still delirious."

Raoule appeared, raising the curtain that hid the bathroom. She was still very slim, very black. Her fingers were refastening the clasp of a necklace.

"It's not true!" cried Jacques, quivering. "I wasn't delirious. It wasn't a dream! Why are you lying to me?"[26]

Raoule took him by the shoulders and made him shrink from her imperious pressure.

"Why does Jacques Silvert speak to me so familiarly? Have I given him permission?"

"Oh! I'm exhausted!" repeated Jacques, trying to pull himself up. "You ought not to mock a man so when he's sick. Raoule! . . . Raoule! I love you! . . . Oh! I think I'm going to die! . . ."

Rambling, crazed, he hid himself in Raoule's arms.

"Is it over?" he added, crying, "Is it really over? . . ."

"I repeat that you . . . had a dream. That's all."

---

[26]Jacques's first use of the *tu* form to Raoule (for which presumption she chastises him in the next line). It is a convention of the nineteenth-century novel that characters sometimes address each other in the *tu* form as a coded way of indicating to readers that they have had sexual relations.

And pushing him away, she turned to the studio, not wanting to hear any more.

"Mademoiselle's dinner is served!" said Marie Silvert, curtseying as if nothing could astonish her. Raoule went to the table, on which a dish was steaming, and placed a pile of gold coins next to a rolled-up napkin.

"This is his place, I believe?" she said very calmly, looking at Marie, who did not flinch.

"Yes, I put you opposite each other."

"Good," replied Raoule, in the same indifferent voice, "I wish you *both* the best of appetites!"

And she walked out, putting her glove back on.

Chapter 5

Raittolbe, realizing at last that Mlle de Vénérande had simply sent an empty carriage to the rendezvous at the Continental, was about to leave after a maddening wait of nine hours, when a cab charged in at the right entrance, Raoule alighted, her veil lowered, a little uneasy, trying to see without being seen.

The baron dashed over, stupefied at her audacity.

"You!" he exclaimed. "This is too much! A yellow carriage instead of a brown one and the right entrance instead of the left. What does this mystification mean? . . ."

"Nothing ought to astonish you, since I'm a woman," Raoule answered, laughing nervously. "I do the complete opposite of what I've promised. What could be more natural!"

"Yes, indeed, what could be more natural! A poor suitor is tortured; he is left to think of horrible things, like an accident, a betrayal, a last-minute change of heart, a family quarrel, or a sudden death, and then he's calmly told: 'What could be more natural?' Raoule, you deserve to go to the police station. I thought that Mlle de Vénérande was loyalty carried to the extreme! Oh! I'm furious!!"

"You will see me home," the young woman said, still smiling. "We'll dine without my aunt, who is plunged into a host of nocturnal devotions these days, and over dinner I'll explain to you . . ."

". . . Indeed! You set me up, I'm sure."

"Get in first, I swear I'll clear everything up afterward, for I deserve my reputation for loyalty, old chap. I could hide things from you, but I won't. Who knows!" (And her face had such a bitter expression that it calmed Raittolbe.) "Who knows if my story won't make up for what you didn't get today!"

He climbed into the brown carriage, very sulky, his mustache bristling, his eyes round like a lion tamer intimidated by his pupil.

During the drive he did not initiate any discussion; *the story* even seemed a bit unnecessary since he was going to dine under Raoule's roof. He knew, and he was not the only one who knew, that in her home Mme Ermengarde's niece remained an unassailable virgin, a kind of goddess who allowed herself everything from a pedestal that no one dared upset. Accordingly he was going to his martyrdom without enthusiasm. Raoule was dreaming with her eyes half closed, gazing through the night she made around her at something very white with all the contours of a human body.

When they reached the mansion, she had a table set and taken into her library, and, while an Etruscan lamp was being placed in the hands of a bronze slave, she sat down on the couch and asked the baron to pull up a comfortable armchair, so graciously that Raittolbe felt capable of strangling his host before touching the soup.[27]

When the dishes had been put on two heated serving tables, Raoule told the footman that they would not need him anymore.

---

[27]The French word for "host" here is *amphitryon*. In Greek mythology, Zeus borrowed the form of Amphitryon in order to seduce Amphitryon's wife, Alcmene (the result was Hercules). In the seventeenth century, Molière, following Plautus, wrote a play that was probably the version of this story most familiar to Rachilde's contemporaries. The plot hinges on the presence of two identical Amphitryons (the real one and Jupiter in his disguise), in which the way to tell them apart is that the real one is a good host. To refer to someone as an amphitryon is thus to compliment them as a good host. In this case, the reference ironically invokes both hospitality and its abuse. Moreover, the reference suggests that Raoule is not herself but is possessed.

"Shall we be quite Regency?"[28] she said.

"Just as you like!" grumbled the baron in a low voice.

A bright fire was burning in the emblazoned fireplace, in a room decorated with tapestry figures that took them back a few centuries, back to the time when the king's supper rose from the floor when he struck it with the handle of his sword. One panel depicted Henri III distributing flowers to his minions.[29] Near Raoule the enameled eyes of an Antinous crowned with vine leaves shone with desire.

Profane names danced along the dark bindings of the books, shelved by the hundreds: Parny, Piron, Voltaire, Boccaccio, Brantôme;[30] and in the midst of the respectable books gaped the doors of an ivory inlaid chest that

---

[28]An allusion to the elegant manners thought to characterize the ancien régime, which included the regency of the duke of Orléans (1715–23).

[29]Henri III of France (1551–89) was famous for his "mignons" (minions or favorites) and is often invoked as a coded reference to male homosexuality.

[30]Writers known for their libertine and gallant subjects: the viscount of Parny (1753–1814) was known for his love poetry; Alexis Piron (1689–1773) wrote satires; Voltaire (1694–1778) was a leading Enlightenment figure; Giovanni Boccaccio (1313–75) is the only non-French example (an Italian), most famous as the author of the *Decameron*, which included bawdy tales; and Pierre de Brantôme (1540–1614) has a special place on the list, since Rachilde's family claimed him as a distant ancestor. The description of this library might be based on the library of Rachilde's grandfather, in which she had free rein as a young girl.

hid between its purple velvet–lined shelves the books no one would admit to having.

Raoule took a ewer and poured herself a goblet of cold water.

"Baron," she said in a tone quivering with both forced gaiety and restrained passion, "I warn you I'll get drunk, because I can't tell my story in a rational fashion. You wouldn't understand it!"

"Ah! Very well!" murmured Raittolbe. "Then I'll try to keep my senses about me!"

And he emptied a whole bottle of Sauternes into an engraved hanap. They examined each other for a moment. To avoid bursting with anger, Raittolbe was forced to admit to himself that Mlle de Vénérande had a face like the most beautiful Diana the huntress.[31]

As for Raoule, she could not see Raittolbe opposite her. The intoxication she mentioned was already filling her eyes, eyes shot with gold.

"Baron," she said brusquely, *"this man is in love!"*

Raittolbe jumped up, set down his hanap, and answered in a choked voice.

---

[31]In addition to evoking the words *veneration* (reverence or worship) and *venereal* (pertaining to physical sex), connotations evident to Anglophone readers, Raoule's family name Vénérande would remind French readers of *la vénérie*, or hunting. Jacques's name is similarly evocative: Silvert is a combination of "sylvan" and "vert" (green).

"Sappho! . . . Of course," he added, with an ironical gesture. "Just as I thought. Go on, M. de Vénérande, go on, my dear *boy*!"

Raoule smiled disdainfully with the corners of her mouth.

"You are mistaken, M. de Raittolbe; if I were Sappho, I would be like everybody else! My upbringing bars me from the crime of schoolgirls and the failings of the prostitute. I think you hold me above the level of ordinary loves? How can you think me capable of such weaknesses? Speak without worrying about convention . . . I'm in my own home here."

The ex-officer of the hussars was trying to bend his fork. He could see that indeed he had fallen headfirst into the sphinx's den. He bowed deeply.

"What on earth was I thinking? Ah! Mademoiselle, forgive me. I was forgetting the *Homo sum* of Messalina!"[32]

"It's true, Monsieur," Raoule went on, shrugging her shoulders, "that I've had lovers. Lovers in my life, like books in my library, to learn, to study . . . But I've never

---

[32]*Homo sum: humani nihil a me alienum puto* ("I am human and therefore I think nothing human alien to me") is a line from the Latin author Terence's play *Heauton Timorunmenos* (translated as "The Self-Tormentor"). But Raittolbe attributes it to Messalina, who was the wife of the emperor Claudius and famous for her debauchery. (She would later become the subject of a work by Rachilde's close friend Alfred Jarry.)

had passion, I haven't written my own book yet! I always found myself alone, when in fact I was two. One is not weak when one remains master of oneself in the midst of the most stupefying pleasures.

"To present my psychological theme under a more . . . Louis XV light,[33] I'd say that although I've read a lot and studied a great deal, I became convinced of the shallowness of my authors, classical or otherwise!

"Now, my heart, that proud scholar, wants to create its little Faust . . . it wants to rejuvenate not its blood but that old-fashioned thing called love!"[34]

"Bravo!" said Raittolbe, convinced that he was about to witness a magical summoning and see a witch pop out of the mysterious chest. "Bravo! I'll help you if I can! Ready at any hour, you know! I too am tired of the eternal chorus that accompanies well-worn procedures. My little Faust, I drink to a new invention and ask only to pay for the patent. By Jove! A brand-new form of love! There's a love that suits me! And yet, Faust, allow me a

---

[33]Louis XV (1710–74) reigned over the age of Enlightenment, when belief in the power of human reason encouraged freedom of thought and the dominance of rationality over passion. This freethinking was often perceived to extend to previously taboo sexual subjects.

[34]Faust sold his soul to the devil in return for the power to realize his wishes (primarily for sexual potency) on earth. Here Rachilde seems to be alluding to part 2 of Goethe's *Faust,* in which a homunculus is produced not through old-fashioned heterosexual reproduction but through pure (cerebral) science.

simple observation. It occurs to me that every woman, when she starts, must think that she has just invented love, because love is only old for us philosophers! It isn't old yet for maidens! Right? Let's be logical!"

She gestured impatiently.

"I represent here," she said, taking a crayfish timbale off the heat, "the elite of the women of our time. An example of the artistic feminine and the grand lady, one of those creatures who revolt at the idea of perpetuating a weakened race or of giving a pleasure they don't share. Well! I come to your tribunal, sent by my sisters, to declare that we all want the impossible, because you love us so badly."

"You have the floor, my dear counsel," insisted Raittolbe, animated but not laughing. "Only I declare that I won't be both judge and defendant. Please put your discourse in the third person: *Because they love us so badly . . .*"

"Yes," Raoule went on, "either brutality or impotence. Such is the choice. The brutal ones exasperate, the impotent ones degrade, and *they* are in such a hurry for their pleasure, both types, that *they* forget to give us, their victims, the only aphrodisiac that could make them happy by making us happy: *Love!* . . ."

"Well!" Raittolbe interrupted, nodding. "Love as aphrodisiac for love! Very pretty! I approve . . . The court is of your opinion!"

"In olden times," the pitiless lady counsel for the defense went on, "vice was sacred, because we were strong; in our own century it's shameful, because it's born of our powerlessness. If one were strong and if one also had grievances against virtue, immorality would be permissible if, for example, one were creative. Sappho would not be a *prostitute* but rather the vestal of a new fire. If I created a new depravity, I would be a priestess, while my imitators would flounder, after my reign, in abominable mud . . . Don't you think that proud men who copy Satan are more guilty than the Satan of Scripture, who invented pride? Isn't Satan respectable precisely because of his sin, which was unprecedented and divinely inspired? . . ."

Raoule, overexcited by a gripping emotion, had risen, her goblet of pure water in her hand. She seemed to be drinking a toast to the Antinous who bent over her.

Raittolbe rose too, filling his hanap with chilled champagne. A little more emotional than a hussar usually is after his tenth glass but more courteous than a rake would have been in the same circumstances, he cried:

"To Raoule de Vénérande, the Christopher Columbus of modern love! . . ." Then, sitting down again: "Counsel, come to the point, because I know that you're *a man in love*, and I don't know why you've betrayed me! . . ."

Raoule resumed painfully:

"A man madly in love! Yes! Already I want to raise an altar to my idol, though I know I'll never be understood! . . . Alas! Can an unnatural passion that is at the same time a real love ever become anything but dreadful madness? . . ."

"Raoule," said the baron de Raittolbe effusively, "I'm certainly convinced that you're a madwoman. But I hope to cure you. Tell me the whole story, and tell me: How, without imitating Sappho, can you be in love with some pretty girl?"

Raoule's pale face turned flame red.

"I'm *a man in love* with a man, not with a woman!" she retorted, while her darkened eyes turned away from the shining eyes of the Antinous. "I've never been loved enough to want to reproduce a being in the image of a husband . . . and I've never been given enough orgasms for my brain not to have had the leisure to look for better . . .

"I wanted the *impossible* . . . It's mine . . . That's to say, no, really . . . it'll never be mine! . . ."

A tear whose wet brightness seemed to have stolen its light from Eden of long ago rolled down Raoule's cheek. As for Raittolbe, he shrugged his shoulders and threw open his arms in a sign of utter despair.

"She's *a man in love* with . . . a ma-a-a-n! Ye Gods!" he exclaimed, "have pity on me! I think my brain is collapsing!"

There was a moment's silence. Then, very slowly, very naturally, Raoule told him how she had first caught sight of Jacques Silvert, how caprice had grown to the size of a wild passion, and how she had bought a human being whom she despised as a man and adored as a *beauty*. (She said "beauty," unable to say "*woman*.")

"Can such a man exist?" the bewildered baron stammered, transported into an unknown world where inversion seemed the only acceptable regime.

"He exists, my friend, and he is not even a hermaphrodite, not even impotent, he is a beautiful twenty-one-year-old male, whose instinctively feminine soul has mistaken its envelope."

"I believe you, Raoule, I believe you! And wouldn't that make you his mistress?" the rake asked, sure that the adventure could have no other outcome.

"I shall be his lover," Mlle de Vénérande answered, still sipping her pure water and crumbling macaroons.

This time Raittolbe burst into hearty laughter.

". . . This is the process I'm ready to pay to patent!" he said.

A severe look stopped him.

"Have you ever denied the existence of Christian martyrs, Raittolbe?"

"Indeed not! I've always had other things to do, my dear Raoule!"

"Do you deny the vocation of the virgin who takes the veil?"

"I yield to evidence. I have a charming cousin at the Carmelites of Moulins."

"Do you deny the possibility of being faithful to an unfaithful wife?"

"For myself, yes, for one of my best friends, no! Ah! Is the water you're drinking enchanted? You frighten me with your questions."

"Well, my dear baron, I'll love Jacques as a fiancé hopelessly loves his dead fiancée!"

They had finished dinner. They pushed back the table that a servant came to remove discreetly, and then, side by side, they stretched out on the couch, each with a Turkish cigarette on the lips.

Raittolbe was not thinking about Raoule's dress and Raoule was not in the least interested in the young officer's mustache.

"So you'll maintain him?" asked the baron in a very noncommittal tone.

"Even if I have to ruin myself! I want *her* to be as happy as a king's *godson!*"

"Let's come to an understanding! If I'm the chief confidant, my dear fellow, let's stick to either *he* or *she* so that I won't lose the few shreds of good sense I have left."

"All right: *She.*"

"And the sister?"

"A servant, that's all!"

"If the ex–flower maker has had a few flings, *she* could have a few more?"

". . . Hashish . . ."

"Damn! It's getting complicated! Suppose, by some odd chance, hashish were not enough?"

"I would kill her!"

At this utterance Raittolbe went and picked up a book at random, feeling the strange need to read aloud to himself. Suddenly, with the help of the rising fumes of champagne, he thought he saw Raoule dressed in the doublet of Henri III, offering a rose to Antinous. His ears buzzed, his temples throbbed. Then, as he choked on the lines that danced before his eyes, he poured out curses dreadful enough to make the hair of all the hussars in France stand on end.

"Be quiet!" Mlle de Vénérande murmured dreamily. "Allow me the chastity of my thoughts when I'm thinking of *her*!"

Raittolbe shook himself. He came over to shake hands with Raoule.

"Good-bye," he said gently. "If I haven't blown my brains out, tomorrow morning we'll go and see her together."

"Your friendship will triumph, my friend! Besides, one can't really be in love with Raoule de Vénérande! . . ."

"Quite right!" Raittolbe replied, and he left very quickly, because vertigo was taking hold of his imagination.

Before going back to her bedroom, Raoule went to see her aunt. She was hunched over a monumental prayer stool, reciting the prayer to the Virgin:

"Remember, sweet Virgin Mary, that no one who has ever sought your intercession has gone unaided . . ."

"Has anyone ever asked her for the grace to change their sex?" wondered the young woman, kissing the pious old woman with a sigh.

Chapter 6

The introduction took place in front of an easel displaying a sketch of a large bouquet of forget-me-nots.

Jacques was wearing his studio outfit: baggy trousers and a flannel jacket.

He had made himself a silk tie by pulling out one of the curtain loops, and, with fresh cheeks and clear eyes, he stood there, very confused by this visit. The fabulous dreams of the hashish, as they passed through his primitive organism, had given him an awkward modesty, a self-conscious shame that showed in all his movements. It was easy to tell from his languid posture that these dreams were haunting his brain, leaving him uncertain of the reality of the fairylike existence he was being made to lead.

Raoule slapped him cavalierly on the shoulder.

"Jacques," she said, "let me introduce one of my friends. He loves good drawings, and you can show him yours."

Raittolbe, strapped into a tight-fitting riding costume and wearing a soldier's high collar, was sniffing ungraciously. As he came in, he had said, "*Wow!*," at the sumptuousness of the apartment.

"Yes," he mumbled, scandalized now by the all too real beauty of the flower maker, "I've done some drawing too, but on staff maps! Does Monsieur paint flowers? . . ."

More and more disconcerted, Jacques glanced reproachfully at Mlle de Vénérande.

"I have done some sheep. Shall I bring them out?" he asked, without directly answering the baron, whose riding whip bothered him. This unexpected submissiveness sent a shiver the length of Raoule's body. She could only nod acquiescence. While he went to look for his drawings, Marie Silvert, draped in a flounced skirt, with a haughty expression and cynical eyes, entered from the bedroom. She wore pinchbeck rings with imitation stones. She stopped short in front of Raittolbe and, forgetting the *sacred* presence of the mistress of the house, cried:

"God! What a good-looking guy!"

Jacques burst out laughing, the dumbfounded baron gaped, and Raoule cast a terrible look.

"My dear, you would do well to keep your admiration to yourself," declared the ex-officer, pointing at Jacques. "There are people here to whom you might suggest evil thoughts! . . ."

That joke, in rather doubtful taste, was meant for the brother, but the sister thought it was addressed to Raoule.

Marie Silvert became very humble, claiming that she had not had a *top-flight* education.

"Now that you are better," Raoule said, haughtily, "you really must get yourself a room next door. It will be more convenient for . . . Jacques! . . ."

"Mademoiselle will be satisfied at once. I realize a servant is out of place among her betters. Yesterday I took a small room on the landing and put a cheap iron bed in there."

Jacques was not listening. He was taking down the picture of the sheep, and the girl backed out, repeating to herself: "What a beau! God! what a beau!"

The incident over, they busied themselves with the drawings of the young artist. In a detached manner,

Raoule told how she had discovered that he had much talent; with a few hours study in the Louvre, her lessons, the deep tranquillity of this isolated neighborhood, he would do wonders and could then compete for the Salon prize. Jacques smiled with his dazzling teeth. Ah, yes! The medal was a noble ambition! Thanks to his benefactress, he would become famous, he would, the poor workman always out of a job!

He spoke slowly, wanting to show Raoule that he knew how to act in good company. From time to time, he turned to Raittolbe, slipping in a *"Don't you agree, sir?"* so shyly that, however disgusted he had been when he arrived, Raittolbe soon felt an immense compassion for this cross-dressed w[hore].

Raoule, stretched out in an armchair, followed Jacques's every movement; when she saw him accept a cigarette, she almost jumped up with rage. He was smoking with shallow intakes, like a child afraid of being burned, then holding it while trying out roguish poses.

"Jacques," Raoule asked, "is your fever gone . . . ?"[35]

He put his cigarette down immediately and blushed. Then she explained to Raittolbe that she spoke familiarly to Silvert because she was older, and in any case studios

---

[35]Raoule slips into using the *tu* form in her question. This accounts for Jacques's blush and the need to explain to Raittolbe.

tolerate such familiarity between fellow artists. The baron nodded his assent. After all, since they were building castles in the air . . . The setting of this monstrous idyll was so thoroughly oriental, the wretchedness of this infamous passion was so cleverly gilded, such a thick carpet had been laid over the mud, that he, the rake, was not so unhappy to be touching these sorry things with the tip of his riding whip! . . .

And, aside from the prostitute and the paramour, he was compromising himself in excellent society.

Although Raittolbe had always been a gentleman till then, the *century weighed on him*, an infirmity impossible to analyze other than by this phrase alone.

He would have much preferred a different hold on Raoule than through the secrets of her private life; but in the end, a beautiful mistress is not unusual, whereas one does not always have the chance to study, in the raw, a new depravity.

Gradually the conversation grew animated. Jacques let himself be won over by the baron's frankness; he said a few amusing things and started confiding things.

"I'll bet that this lad who isn't big enough to be a soldier has had some mighty big affairs with women instead? . . ." Raittolbe ventured, winking.

"With his phiz! No doubt! . . . ," added Raoule, nervously kneading one of her gloves.

81

"Oh, no! . . . I swear," said Jacques, a little astonished that such a question should be asked in such a place. "If I've *spent the night* ten times," and he winked back at Raittolbe, "that's all, really! . . ."

Raoule rose to modify something in the sketch of the blue bouquet.

"No flings? No intrigues?" insisted the baron.

"Only the rich have the right to be in love!" muttered the flower maker, suddenly losing his gaiety.

Down to the ash of his cigarette, Raittolbe complimented Jacques on his fine talent, bowed to him as to a woman in her own home, that is, with exaggerated respect, and then took his leave of Raoule, saying briefly to her: "At the Italiens,[36] this evening, right? . . ."

She shook her head, without turning around, and called to Jacques.

"Here, stupid," she said, slapping him with her shredded gloves, "try to put some life into your wretched forget-me-nots! You are still thinking too much about your former job. You paint wooden flowers!"

"I'll start over, Mademoiselle, since they're intended for your aunt."

"Oh well, if they're for my aunt, you can make them like marble if you want!"

---

[36]Popular name for Offenbach's opéra comique on the boulevard of the same name.

Raittolbe had gone.

"I forbid you to smoke!" she cried, shaking Jacques by the arm.

"All right! I won't do it again!"

"And I forbid you to speak to a man here without my permission."

Jacques, taken aback, stood still, keeping his stupid smile.

Suddenly she jumped at him, and threw him down at her feet before he had time to struggle; then grasping his neck, which his white flannel jacket left bare, she dug her nails into his flesh.

"I am *a jealous man!*" she roared madly. "Do you understand me now? . . ."

Jacques did not move, he had put his clenched fists, which he did not want to use against her, in his tear-filled eyes.

Sensing that she was hurting him, Raoule relaxed.

"You must see," she said ironically, "that my hands unlike yours are not those of a flower maker, and that, of the two of us, I'm always the more manly!"

Jacques did not answer, but looked at her from the corner of his eye, a bitter smile playing at each corner of his lips.

His feminine beauty was all the more apparent in this imposed inertia, and from his weakness, perhaps now voluntary, there emanated a mysteriously attractive power.

"How cruel you are! . . . ," he said very quietly.

Raoule snatched a cushion at random and placed it under the young man's red head.

"You drive me crazy!" she stammered. "I want you for myself alone, and yet you talk, you laugh, you listen, you answer in front of others with the poise of an ordinary being! Don't you see that your almost supernatural beauty debauches the mind of all who approach you?

"Yesterday, I wanted to love you in my own way without explaining my sufferings; today, I'm out of my mind because one of my friends sat next to you! . . ."

She was interrupted by raucous sobs and tried to hide her face from him with her handkerchief.

On bended knees beside his outstretched body, she had a lover's fury that burned Jacques in spite of himself; so he sat up to put an arm around her shoulders.

"So you love me very much? . . . ," he asked, cynical and sweetly cajoling at the same time.[37]

"To die for! . . ."

"Will you promise me to make me delirious all day long again? . . ."

"Do you prefer that delirium to my kisses, Jacques?"

---

[37]Jacques also slips back into the *tu* form at this point.

"No! . . . and your remedy won't intoxicate me again, so there, because I'll spit it out if you force it down my throat! . . . It will be a different, a better delirium. . ."

He stopped, a little breathless, surprised at having said so much, and then went on speaking in a tone that seemed to quiver with voluptuous ardor: "Why did you come with that gentleman? . . . Can't I be jealous too? You cause me terrible shame! You've bought me and you beat me . . . it's as if I were a little dog! If you think I can't see it! I should have left, but there it is . . . Your green jam has made me more cowardly than my sister!

"I'm afraid of everything . . . And yet I'm happy, very happy . . . I'm like a six-week-old baby again, and I want to sleep on my nurse's breast . . ."

Raoule was kissing his golden hair, as fine as gauzy thread, trying to blow her monster passion in through his skull. Her imperious lips made him bend his head forward, and she bit him full on the nape of his neck.

Jacques twisted with a cry of amorous pain.

"Oh! that feels good!" he sighed, stiffening in the arms of his wild dominatrix. "I don't want anything else! Raoule, you can love me as you please, provided you always caress me like that!"

The studio draperies were lowered. The noise of the buses and carriages passing in the street grew fainter through the double windows; only a distant rumbling like that of an express train could be heard. Near the big day bed against which Raoule had thrown Jacques fell an intimate half light, and the cushions piled up behind them seemed like the padded compartment of a luxury train . . . They were alone, carried off in a terrifying vertigo that shifted everything around . . . they were plunging toward bottomless pits and thought they were safe in each other's arms.

"Jacques," replied Raoule, "I have made *a god* of our love. Our love shall be eternal . . . My caresses will never cease!"

"Then it's true you find me beautiful? That you find me worthy of you, most beautiful of women? . . ."

"You are so beautiful, dear creature, that you are more of a belle than I! Look there in the mirror, at your pink and white neck, like a child's neck! . . . Look at your marvelous mouth like the wound in a fruit ripened in the sun! Look at the light pouring from your deep, pure eyes like the full light of day . . . Look! . . ."

She pulled him up a little, pushing aside with her feverish fingers his clothes on his chest.

"Jacques, don't you know that fresh and healthy flesh is the only power in this world! . . ."

He shuddered. His masculinity awoke with these soft words spoken low.

She was not striking him now, she was not buying him, she was not flattering him, and the male, however abject he may be, always possesses, at some moment of revolt, that ephemeral virility called *fatuity*.

"You have proved to me," he said, squeezing her waist with a bold smile, "you have indeed proved to me that I didn't have to blush before you, Raoule. The blue bed is waiting for us, come! . . ."

A cloud descended from Raoule's hair to cover her scowling forehead.

"All right . . . but on one condition, Jacques? You won't be my lover . . ."

He began to laugh openly, as he would have laughed if he had met a recalcitrant whore in a certain kind of house.

"I won't dream this time? That must be what you mean, you wicked thing! . . . ," he said, pulling away with the ease of a young deer who is released.

"You'll be my slave, Jacques, if one can call the delightful abandonment of your body to me slavery."

Jacques tried to drag her after him, but she resisted.

"Do you swear it? . . . ," she questioned, in a tone grown imperious once again.

"What? . . . You are mad! . . ."

"Am I the master, yes or no!" cried Raoule, suddenly drawing herself up with hard eyes and flaring nostrils.

Jacques backed away to the easel.

"I'm leaving . . . I'm leaving!" he repeated in despair, no longer understanding his master's desires, and not desiring anything any longer himself.

"You won't leave, Jacques. You've given yourself away, and you can't take yourself back! Are you forgetting that we love each other? . . ."

This love was now almost a threat; so he turned his back on her, sulking.

But she came up behind him; she caught him up in her lascivious arms.

"Sorry!" she muttered, "I was forgetting that you're a capricious little woman, with the right, *in her own home*, to torture me.

"Come on! . . I'll do whatever you want . . ."

They went to the blue bedroom, he stunned by her furious demand for the impossible, she with cold eyes and biting her delicate lip. It was she who undressed herself, refusing all his advances and causing him terrible anxiousness. Without the slightest coquetry she took off her dress and her corset. Then she lowered the curtains, preventing him from admiring her splendid amazonian figure. When he kissed her, it seemed to him that a body made of marble had slid between the sheets; he had the disagreeable sensation that a dead animal was brushing against his own warm limbs.

"Raoule," he begged, "don't call me a *woman* again, it's humiliating . . . and you can see that I can't be anything but your lover? . . ."

The blasé woman, on the pillows, shrugged imperceptibly in a way that signaled her complete indifference.

"Raoule," Jacques repeated, trying to animate with furious kisses the mouth that a while ago had been so passionate, the mouth of the one he believed his mistress. "Raoule! don't scorn me, I beg you . . . We love each other, you said so yourself . . . Oh! I'm going crazy . . . I feel I'm dying . . . There are things I'll never do . . . never . . . Until I have you all to myself and with all your heart!"

Raoule's eyes closed. She knew that game, she knew word for word what nature would say with Jacques's voice . . .

How many times had she heard such cries, howls from some, sighs from others, polite preambles from the seasoned ones, hesitant starts from the shy ones . . . ? And when they had all had a good shout, when they had all finally obtained the realization of their dearest desires, in the timeworn phrase, they all became happily sated, all equally vulgar in the appeasement of their senses.

"Raoule," Jacques stammered, falling back exhausted by hopeless pleasure. "Do what you like with me now, I can see that the vice-ridden don't know how to love! . . ."

The young woman's body vibrated from head to foot when she heard the wrenching cry of this man who was only a child when compared to her cursed knowledge. With a single leap, she jumped on him and covered him with her flanks swollen by savage ardor.

"I . . . Raoule de Vénérande, I don't know how to love! . . . Don't say that, because I know how to wait! . . ."

Chapter 7

The man seated on her right in the clouds of some imaginary heaven has relegated his female companion to the second rung in the scale of beings.

In that, male instinct has prevailed. The inferior role that her form imposes on women in the generative act evidently gives rise to an idea of the yoke of slavery.

Man possesses, woman submits.

The emotional faculties of the former do not go beyond the limits of his physical power. When procreation has done its work, calm descends on him. Nothing survives past the sensual paroxysm.

For the latter, on the contrary, brutal manifestations idealize the flesh, the action of the senses extends to the intellectual domain, the imagination awakens to limitless aspirations.

All is said and done for man, who collapses sated, broken, annihilated, and yet, avid for embraces, calling for more caresses, bringing forth new joys. At his side, woman prostitutes herself to conceptions of paradise.

Man is matter; pleasure is woman, the eternally unappeased.

Is it not in this profound disparity, this monstrous antithesis, that we should look for the secrets of passion without procreation, the sole fruit of couplings that know no name?

Forget natural law, tear up the procreative pact, deny the subordination of the sexes, then we shall understand the incredible excesses of that other prostitute, pagan antiquity.

What passion today described as vice or monstrosity was not then celebrated, consecrated with incense, deified? Olympus is populated with bastard gods who all had their poets, their followers, their priests.

Beneath the shroud of extinct generations—Rome, Athens, Lesbos—accursed joys still groan.

Sweet Catullus, pious Vergil, inconsolable Sappho, pleasure-loving Horace, and so many others,[38] are they not still singing for us of these mystic passions that man, keen to take back his full imperial authority, has since reproved without ever being able to extinguish them?

---

[38]Catullus (87–54 BC), Vergil (70–19 BC), and Horace (65–8 BC) made reference in their work to forms of love that were considered deviant in terms of the medical and sexological paradigms that would have been familiar to Rachilde's ninteenth-century readers.

Born of dreams, they escape the common yoke. Their ascendance is immortal, like the material they transform through idealization!

The seal of infamy is forever broken. Each day brings a new guest to the great orgy. Ephebes and mad virgins multiply. The inebriation mounts.

Modern civilization, a worthy offspring of the one that gave birth to it, in the midst of silence and solitude, repeats the hymn of the saturnalia.[39]

Now, as before, man has depleted his force, smashed his scepter. Feminized, like the ancient Ephebe, he lies at the feet of Pleasure.

Pleasure is a woman.

In the radiance of a vengeful dawn, woman shall glimpse the possibility of a fabulous fall for man.

She will invent caresses, she will find new proofs in the new transports of a new love, and Raoule de Vénérande will possess Jacques Silvert . . .

Chapter 8

A strange life began for Raoule de Vénérande, starting with the fatal moment when Jacques Silvert gave up his power as a man in love and became her thing, a sort of

---

[39]The Saturnalia was an ancient Roman festival honoring Saturn characterized by licentiousness, debauchery, and disorder.

lifeless object who let himself be loved, because his own love was powerless. For Jacques loved Raoule with a real woman's heart. He loved her out of gratitude, out of submission, out of a latent desire for unknown pleasures. He had the same passion for her that one has for hashish, and now he much preferred her to the green jam. The degrading habits she had taught him had become a natural necessity.

They saw each other almost every day, as often as Raoule's social obligations allowed.

When she had no visits, soirées, or studies, she would jump into a cab and arrive at the boulevard Montparnasse with the key to the studio in her hand. She would give some brief orders to Marie, and often a royally filled purse, and then she would shut herself in their temple, isolated from the rest of the world. Jacques very rarely asked to go out. When she did not come, he worked or read all kinds of books, science or literature pell-mell, whatever Raoule furnished him to keep his primitive mind under her spell.

He led the lazy existence of oriental women confined to the harem who know nothing except love and for whom everything comes back to love.

Sometimes there were scenes with his sister about his passivity. She would have liked him to have a household, other mistresses, and the desire to squander the wealth of the sinful woman. But he, always calm, declared that she could not understand, that she would never understand.

Besides, the portieres kept Marie from looking through the keyhole. She was obliged in effect to remain a stranger to the mysteries of the blue chamber. Raoule came and went, commanded, acted like a man well past his first affair, although this was his first love. She forced Jacques to bask in his passive happiness like a pearl in its shell. The more he forgot his sex, the more she created around him multiple opportunities to feminize himself, and, so as not to frighten too much the male inside him that she wanted to smother, she treated each degrading idea at first as a joke, content to make him accept it seriously only later. Thus, one morning she sent him via her footman an enormous bouquet of white flowers, with this note: "I picked this perfumed armful of flowers for you in my greenhouse. Don't scold me, I am sending flowers instead of kisses. A fiancé could not do better! . . ."

Jacques turned very red when the flowers arrived, then he solemnly placed the flowers in pots around the studio, playing out the game with himself, catching himself being a woman for the pleasure of art.

At the beginning of their relationship, he would have felt grotesque. With the excuse that he wanted to breathe some fresh air he would have gone out, would have gone to the club next door for a glass of beer in the company of salesmen and casual laborers.

Raoule noticed at once the change she had wrought in that weak character, when she saw the way her bouquet had been arranged, and every morning thereafter her footman was sent to leave immaculate white flowers with Jacques's concierge.

Why white, why immaculate?

Jacques did not ask.[40]

---

[40]Jacques does not ask, but the reader may well wonder. One possibility is that Rachilde was alluding to the popular novel *La dame aux camélias* by Alexandre Dumas fils (1848), the story about a courtesan with a heart of gold that later served as the basis for Verdi's opera *La traviata*. In the second chapter of this novel, a brief paragraph explains that Marguerite got her nickname because she was never seen without a bunch of camellias. The next paragraph in its entirety reads: "For twenty-five days of the month, the camellias were white, and for five they were red; no one ever discovered the reason for this variation in color, which I note without being able to explain it, and which the habitués of the theaters where she went most frequently and her friends had also noticed" (32). The worldly narrator of Dumas's novel is unable to explain the color code, but that the cycle is explicitly monthly, along with the symbolic colors (the purity of white, the association of red with blood), suggests that Marguerite uses the flowers to let her admirers know when they are not welcome because of her menstrual cycle. In *Monsieur Vénus*, Jacques does not want to think too hard about what it might mean that Raoule sends him only white flowers, but one possible interpretation is that Raoule never menstruates. In addition to underscoring her virilization, the absence of menstruation means that she will never conform to gender expectations that femininity be manifested through reproduction and childbirth. Alternatively, since Jacques occupies the role of the courtesan in this novel, his biological maleness means he will never menstruate, so Raoule can be sure that white flowers will always be appropriate.

One day, toward the end of May, Raoule ordered a closed carriage and took Jacques for an afternoon drive in the Bois.

He was as happy as a schoolboy on holiday, but he enjoyed this strange favor very discreetly. He stayed back in the carriage, close to her, his head falling on her shoulder, repeating those adorable nothings that made his beauty still more provocative.

With her forefinger, through the closed window, Raoule pointed out to him the principal people passing near them. She explained to him the *high-life*[41] terms she was using and told him about a world that appeared forbidden to him, a poor monster without a conscience.

"Ah!" he would say, cuddling up to her, frightened, "someday you'll marry and you'll leave me!" Which gave him, so fresh, so blond, the touching charm of a seduced young girl who glimpses the possibility of being forgotten.

"No, I shall never marry!" Raoule asserted. "No, I'll never leave you, Jaja, and if you are good, you'll always be mine! . . ."[42]

They would both laugh, but they were more and more united in a common thought: the destruction of their sex.

---

[41]The word is in English in the original French.
[42]In this exchange, Jacques uses *tu*, while Raoule switches to *vous*.

Jaja, however, had whims, attainable whims. He disappointed his sister, whose hopes went far beyond the studio stuffed with glad rags. He asked for a pretty dressing gown of blue velvet, lined with blue . . . and it was with his heels catching in the long hem of this garment that he greeted Raoule at the door. She came once, about midnight, dressed in a man's suit, a gardenia in her buttonhole, her hair hidden in curls, a top hat, her riding hat, low on her forehead. Jacques had fallen asleep; he had read a lot while waiting for her and in the end let the book slip from his fingers. The night-light shed a mysterious glow over the bed of silky brocade, ornamented with Venetian lace. His tousled head lay on the fine linen of the sheet with a charming softness. His shirt buttoned to the neck revealed nothing of the man, and his rounded, completely hairless arm stood out like beautiful marble on the satin counterpane.

Raoule looked at him for a minute, wondering with a kind of superstitious terror if she, like God, had not created a being in her own image. She touched him with the tip of her glove. Jacques awoke, stammering a name, but seeing this young man standing beside his bed, he jumped, shouting in terror:

"Who are you? What do you want? . . ."

Raoule took off her hat with a respectful gesture.

"Madame sees before her the most humble of her adorers," she said, bending at the knee.

For a moment he hesitated, with haggard eyes going from her patent-leather boots to her short brown curls.

"Raoule! Raoule! . . . Is it possible? you'll get arrested! . . ."

"Nonsense, foolish girl! Because I come in without ringing the bell?"

He held out his arms to her, and she smothered him with passionate kisses, stopping only when she saw him swooning, unable to go on, begging for the ultimate realization of an artificial pleasure that he endured as much from a need for satisfaction as for the love of the sinister courtesan.

He got used to the nocturnal disguise, no longer believing that a dress was indispensable to Raoule de Vénérande.

Since he had a very vague idea of the life of the *high and mighty*, as his sister often called them, it never occurred to him what efforts of ingenuity Raoule had to make in order to leave the courtyard of her mansion without being noticed.

Aunt Ermengarde was always asleep by eight o'clock on evenings when there were no guests to receive. But after tea on Saturday all the servants went to and fro between the hall and the drawing room, so that, in order to leave her room by the back stairs, Raoule had to take the most minute precautions. However, one evening when the big chandelier in the drawing room had just been put out, as she started down, she met a man who was lighting his cigar. To turn back was to lose her opportunity, to go out was to risk giving herself away . . . She went on, passing close to the man, who touched the brim of his hat, not without looking at her very attentively.

"Just a minute, sir," the straggler murmured, touching her shoulder. "Could you give me a light?"

Raoule had recognized Raittolbe.

"Well," she said, accentuating her haughty look, "you are venturing into the chambermaids' quarters, dear chap."

"What about you?" the ex-officer shot back, very much piqued.

"That's none of your business, I imagine."

"Yes, sir, it is," he replied, "because this way one can also reach the apartments of a lady for whom I have the deepest respect. Mlle de Vénérande's room is just above us, I think. I shall give you my explanation in return for yours. Mlle Jeanne's face brought me here. It is stupid, but it is true . . . Your turn now."

"Such impertinence," said Raoule, smothering her desire to laugh.

Raittolbe promptly threw his card and his cigar in Raoule's face, and, despite the peril, she burst out laughing.

She took off her hat and turned her beautiful face to her interlocutor.

"Well, for heavens sake!" Raittolbe grumbled, "that's a masquerade I wasn't expecting!"

"Too bad . . . I'll take you with me! . . . ," Raoule replied, and they reached the tilbury that was waiting in the avenue. Raittolbe expatiated in lamentations on depraved women who spoil the best things. He declared that this young Jacques looked to him like a parcel of rotten flesh. As for his sister, she had good reasons to love handsome young men. Indeed! She was at least upholding the honor of her guild. Thus muttering and cursing, he steered the horse toward the boulevard Montparnasse, while Raoule, leaning back, laughed heartily. They arrived very late.

A woman under a street lamp appeared to be waiting for them in silence, opposite Notre-Dame-des-Champs.

There were very few people in the street at such an hour, and one might have well taken her for a streetwalker.

"Psst! . . . Want to come up to my place? The gentleman with the decoration . . . I am as nice as the next one, you know," the prostitute said, accosting Raittolbe.

She was wearing a silk dress, with a Spanish mantilla held by a coral comb. Her eyes shone with promises, though a hollow cough had interrupted her sentence.

"So it's you . . ." exclaimed Mlle de Vénérande, raising her riding whip with one hand and seizing the woman's arm with the other.

Marie Silvert, seeing that she was recognized by the master of the house, tried to backtrack.

"'Scuse me," she stammered, "I thought you were some acquaintance of mine, you know. Don't take it wrong, I know some swells as well."

Raoule struck Marie impetuously on the temple, and since the riding whip had a little round agate handle, Marie Silvert fell unconscious upon the pavement.

"Oh, hell!" said Raittolbe, exasperated. "You might have restrained your indignation, my young friend; we'll be taken to the police station, for sure! Not to mention, you are illogical. If you come down in the world, she goes up . . . Punishment was unnecessary!"

Raoule shivered.

"Hush, Raittolbe! My passion has nothing to do with this low-grade female. I should have thrown her out long ago."

"I don't advise you to try! . . ." the ex-officer of hussars replied dryly.

He picked Marie up, slung her over a shoulder, and before the police could arrive, they were admitted to the house.

Raoule, not worrying about how the adventure might turn out for Raittolbe, let him enter the sister's room while she went to the brother's. Jacques had not gone to bed, and he had even heard shouts in the street.[43]

He ran to Raoule and threw himself on her neck, just as an anxious wife would have done.

"Jaja not happy," he declared, in a tone whose naïveté was belied by his cheeky smile.

"Why's that, my treasure?" And Raoule almost carried him to the nearest armchair.

"I thought you were being arrested, really I did; there was a fight, I think, right outside my window."

"No, nothing! By the way, you hadn't told me that your esteemed sister isn't satisfied with the comfort I give her. She accosts passersby on the boulevard at one o'clock in the morning."

"Oh!" said Jacques, scandalized.

"Mistaking me for someone else just now, she allowed herself . . ."

Such an idea would have amused the flower maker three months before, but that evening it made him indignant . . .

"The wretch!" he said.

---

[43]The essence of the situation described here would later become the subject of Rachilde's one-act play *La voix du sang*. A complacent, bourgeois couple hear the sounds of someone's being attacked in the street but choose not to intervene or help. The play's tragic denouement reveals that it was their son who was attacked and that he will die because no one came to his aid.

"You will allow me to get rid of Mlle Silvert, won't you?"

"You are within your rights! To accost you? . . . ," he said in a jealous tone.

"Obviously I must look like a gentleman . . . a prospect, as these ladies say!" And Raoule put down her overcoat with masculine informality.

"And yet," Jacques sighed, "you will always be lacking one thing!"

She sat at his feet on a low stool, adoring him in mute ecstasy. He wore his velvet dressing gown tied tightly around his waist with a silk cord, and his shirt, with embroidered front, had just enough collar to avoid being a completely feminine garment. His hands, of which he took great care, were a flat white like the hands of a lady of leisure. On his red hair he had sprinkled brilliantine.

"You are divine! . . . ," said Raoule. "Have I ever seen you so pretty?"

"It's because I have a complete surprise for you . . . We're going to have supper! . . . I've ordered champagne, and I've decided to be annoying!"

"Really?"

He pushed back the Chinese screen and revealed to Raoule a table set with an ice bucket at each end.

"There!" he said. "I even want to make you drunk!"

"So, Mademoiselle is at home!"

Just then someone pounded on the door.

"Who's there?" asked Jacques, very irritated.

"Me!" Marie shot back. And, when they had unbolted the door, she entered, very pale, her mantilla torn off, some blood on her cheek.

"My God! What's the matter?" Jacques cried out.

"Oh, nothing," the woman said in a hoarse voice . . . "Madame almost killed me, that's all!"

"Killed you!"

"Let's all calm down!" said Raoule contemptuously. "There must be a doctor in the neighborhood; have the concierge fetch him or send Raittolbe, if he hasn't already left."

"Here I am," said the latter, appearing and nodding to Raoule, who did not move.

"Explain yourself," murmured Jacques, pouring out a glass of champagne for his sister and making her sit in an armchair.

"Here's the thing, my boy. That hussy you love backward beat me up, on the pretext that I was soliciting at her door. We are not in our own home here, it seems ! . . .

"If it weren't for her, it would be carnival night every night, you see! She's going to meddle with the affairs of poor girls who have different tastes from hers. She plays the vice squad, writes up their tickets, and beats them up into the bargain.

"But in spite of this gentleman's honesty"—and Marie pointed to the baron, who was still making desperate signs to Raoule—"I'm going to settle with her right away. I don't care a rap about your filthy love, but as long as we are rabble together, we can shake it up a bit before we part company, can't we!"

Spluttering out these words, which crackled like rifle shots across the splendors of the room, the girl rolled up her sleeves and, rising from the armchair, came and planted herself in front of Raoule.

She was completely drunk. When her breath reached Mlle de Vénérande's face, it seemed to the latter that a bottle of alcohol was being poured over her.

"Miserable wretch," roared Raoule, searching her pockets for the dagger that never left her side.

Raittolbe threw himself between them, while Jacques held his sister back.

"That's enough!" said Raittolbe, who wished he were a thousand leagues away from the boulevard Montparnasse. "You are very ungrateful, Mlle Silvert, and what's more, you are not in your right senses. Please leave!"

"No," roared Marie, absolutely beside herself, "I want to take down the slut before I go. She disgusts me, I tell you."

Jacques, in consternation, kept trying to push her outside.

"You too," she yelled, "disown your sister, you filthy f[ag]!"

Jacques turned as pale as death; and slowly, without a word in answer, he went to his room, and let the portiere fall behind him. At last, Raittolbe, his patience exhausted, seized Marie bodily and, in spite of her struggles and furious cries, carried her to her room and locked her in. Then he came back to Raoule:

"My dear friend," he said, trying not to look her in the face, "I think this scene gives you something to think about; this creature, however defiled she may be, looks very dangerous to me . . . take care! If you chase her away, in two days everyone in Paris who is anyone may know the story of Jacques Silvert."

"Will you, instead of that, help me to crush her?" Raoule asked, livid with rage.

"My dear child! You don't know what a real female is like. For her, no change is possible. I promise to calm her, that's all!"

"By what means?" asked Raoule, frowning.

"That's my secret; but you can be sure your friend will be assiduous."

Raoule drew back, revolted; she understood.

"One does what one can," said Raittolbe, and he left in a very dignified manner.

Chapter 9

"Since we are all rabble together," Marie Silvert had said . . . These words kept Raoule from loving for the rest of the night. All the souvenirs of Greek grandeur with which she surrounded her modern idol were suddenly pushed aside like a veil blown by the wind, and the daughter of the Vénérandes glimpsed ignoble things whose existence she had never even suspected. In love all women are linked by the same chain . . .

The honest wife, when she gives herself to her legal husband, is in the same position as the prostitute when she gives herself to her lover.

Nature has made these victims naked, and society gives them only clothes. Without clothes there is no distance between them, only the difference in physical beauty; there, sometimes, it is the prostitute who wins.

Christian philosophers have spoken of purity of intention, but they have never called that last point into question during the amorous struggle . . . At least we don't think so! They would have found it too distracting.

Raoule thus saw herself on the same level as the ex-prostitute . . . and, although she might have the superiority of beauty, she did not have that of pleasure: she gave it but did not receive it.

All monsters have their moments of weariness, and she was weary . . . Jacques cried.

At dawn, she left the studio, took a cab, and went back to her mansion.

While waiting for lunch, she fenced with one of her cousins, a stupid snob, but he looked good while fencing, and then she discussed with her aunt the prospects of some travel. Raoule thought they should leave at once, to get a jump on the spa season. The canoness countered that she had charity visits to pay, farm accounts to settle, and a cook to replace. Wealth is sometimes very trying, society very tiresome, and the world full of tribulations.

However, the new Sappho could not yet take the Leucadian jump.[44] A piercing pain from the depths of her being warned her that her idol still clung to a perishable

---

[44]Although the name of Sappho is most often associated with female homosexuality today, from antiquity until the end of the nineteenth century the association with female same-sex love was often suppressed in favor of a heterosexual notoriety: it was commonly rumored that Sappho committed suicide for the love of a man (Phaon) by jumping into the Aegean Sea from a cliff on the island of Leucas, and this aspect of the Sappho story would have been well known to Rachilde's contemporaries. For a thorough analysis of how Sappho has been interpreted through the ages, see DeJean.

being. Like inventors stopped by some obstacle on the threshold of perfecting their discoveries, she hoped, in spite of the mud, to see in Jacques's bright eyes another corner of her heaven that she could again fill with dreams.

Three days went by. Jacques did not write. Marie did not come. As for Raittolbe, he kept an absolute neutrality. One evening Raoule, exasperated by the uncertainty, put on her man's suit and ran to the boulevard Montparnasse. As she entered, she met Marie Silvert, who greeted her with an obsequious smile and withdrew, without showing in her attitude anything that might recall what had happened between them. Jacques was making elaborate initials on some writing paper. It was an order placed by Raoule, who had paid him in advance with passionate kisses.

A delightful calm reigned in the studio, and the light of the lamp with its lowered shade fell only on Jacques's adorable face. This was certainly not the face of an abject person; everything in his features indicated rather the candor of a virgin contemplating the priesthood. A little uneasy at the sight of Raoule, he laid down his pencil and stood up.

"Jacques," said Raoule quietly, "you are a coward, my friend."

Jacques fell back into his armchair. A deathly pallor spread from his forehead to his neck.

"Your sister's epithets the other night were crude but accurate."

He grew still paler.

"You are kept by a woman, you work only to have something to do, and you accept a loathsome situation without the slightest revolt."

Frightened, he looked up at her.

"I think," Raoule went on, "that it's not Marie whom I should dismiss as a vile creature."

Jacques pressed his fingers to his breast, for he was suffering.

"You will leave here," Raoule added just as coldly, "you will go and seek work from an engraver. I'll help you to gain entry, and then you'll go back to your garret and try to regain the dignity of a man."

Jacques rose again.

"Yes," he said, brokenly, "I will obey you, Mademoiselle. You're right."

"On these conditions," Raoule went on, more gently, "I promise you a reward such as you have never dreamt of."[45]

---

[45]In this exchange, both Jacques and Raoule use the *vous* form, underscoring that they are role-playing, but Raoule switches to *tu* in the subsequent conversation, while Jacques continues in the *vous* form until the line "No, I assure you, it's over."

"What, Mademoiselle?" he asked while putting his tools in order on the mat of his rosewood desk.

"I'll make you my husband."

Jacques drew back, raising his arms.

"Your husband?"

"Of course! I ruined you, and I will rehabilitate you. Nothing simpler! Our love is only a degrading torture that you submit to because I pay you. Well, I give you back your freedom. I hope that you'll manage to use it to win me all over again . . . if you love me."

Jacques leaned on the easel behind him.

"Well, I refuse," he said bitterly.

"What! You refuse to marry me?"

"I refuse to rehabilitate myself, even at that price."

"Why?"

"Because I love you, as you have taught me to love you . . . and I want to be a coward, and I want to be vile, and the torture you talk about is my life now. I'll go back to a garret, if you insist, I'll be poor again, I'll work, but when you want me, I'll still be your slave, the one you call my wife!"

A thunderbolt landing in front of her would not have taken Raoule more aback.

"Jacques! Jacques! Have you forgotten our first embraces, then? Just think of it! To be my husband, for you, once a penniless workman, is to be a king!"

111

"Well!" Jacques muttered, two big tears in his eyes, "it's not my fault if I don't feel up to it anymore!"

Raoule rushed to him with open arms:

"Oh! I love you," she cried, transported with pleasure. "Yes, I'm crazy; I think I even just asked you something unnatural . . . Dearest darling . . . Forget it, you're better than I could have imagined."

She led him to the couch and, as it often amused her to do, sat him on her knee. They looked like two brothers reconciled.

"A pretty sight, indeed, I would be dressed in white, with the veil of a modest bride on my forehead . . . I who hate to be ridiculous . . . But, look here, are you being serious, darling idiot, you really don't care to? . . ."

Jacques was sobbing, his head in the crook of Raoule's elbow.

"No, I assure you, it's over. I'll take what you want to give me, and if I had to change, there are times when I would refuse. Only, if you knew how much I love you, you wouldn't insult me, you'd take great pity on me instead. I'm very unhappy."

She held him tightly, rocking him in her arms, calming him like a baby. This triumph, won despite her own conscience, was intoxicating her all over again. The coarse insults of the prostitute no longer rang in her ears. Once again, Greek images were surrounding her idol in a cloud of incense. Now it was love for the love of vice; Jacques was becoming God.

She wiped his cheeks and questioned him about his sister.

"I don't know anything about the life she leads," he replied in a sulky voice; "she's always out, and in the evening she's always expecting someone. I think it's the baron you introduced to me one day."

"Impossible," Raoule exclaimed, bursting into laughter . . . "Raittolbe lowering himself to that extent! . . . After all, she's free, so is he, but I forbid you to worry about it."

"Do you forgive her for the scene she made the other day? You know she was drunk . . ."

"I forgive her since, indirectly, she's the cause of the talk we've just had. I'd go to hell, if I thought that's where I could find the proof of your sincere love, my little Jacques!"

He lay down at her feet and kissed them with passionate humility . . . then he sighed, "I'm sleepy," as he put the pointy heels of Raoule's shoes on his forehead.

She made him get up, for she had understood.

That night Raoule, who was to take part in a hunt the next day, at the duchess of Armonville's, near Fontainebleau, left about one, leaving Jacques sound asleep.

She was on her way downstairs when Jacques's door was opened cautiously: a man in his shirtsleeves burst into the blue room, which he took in at a glance.

"M. Silvert," he said then, sure that he and Jacques were alone in the room, "M. Silvert, I wish to speak to you; get up, and let's go into the studio."

It was the baron de Raittolbe; his disheveled appearance showed plainly that he had left the other half of his clothes not too far away. He seemed very much annoyed to find himself there, but an irrevocable resolution shone under his thick black eyebrows. In the end, he was thoroughly revolted by all that he had seen and heard. In this sad situation, he thought that his influence as a truly virile man should make itself felt. Since he had been drawn into the matter, he would take advantage of the fact to stop things from moving any faster.

"Jacques!" he repeated loudly, approaching the bed.

The glow of the night-light slunk along the rounded shoulders of the sleeper and went in a caressing flow to the ends of his feet.

He had fallen naked, shattered by fatigue on the rumpled bedspread whose blue satin made his ruddy skin more dazzling. His head was buried in his crooked arm, so white that it had pearly tints. In the hollow of his back a golden shadow emphasized the splendid suppleness of his rump, and one of his legs, spread a little apart from the other, twitched like that of a nervous woman whose senses have been overstimulated. Around his wrists two gold bangles, with constellations of diamonds, sparkled under the azured sheets that had fallen on him, and a bottle of attar of roses, lying in an indentation of the pillow, was spreading a heady perfume like all the loves of the Orient.

The baron de Raittolbe, standing before this disorderly bed, had a strange hallucination. The former officer of hussars, the brave duelist, the joyful rake, who held in equal esteem a pretty girl and an enemy's bullet, swayed for half a second: instead of the blue all around him he saw red, his mustache bristled, his teeth clenched, a shiver ran the length of his body, followed by a cold sweat. He was almost frightened.

"I'll be damned," he muttered, "if it isn't Eros himself. I'll see him decorated for the public good."

And, like an amateur sometimes interested in a military review, he ran his eyes over the sculptured outlines of this flesh that was spreading warm emanations of desire.

"Now's the time, I think, to pick up a bludgeon," he added, trying to shake off his admiration.

"Jacques!" he roared, loudly enough to shake the room to the ceiling.

Jacques sat up; but, though he had been awakened abruptly, he appeared graceful in his stupor; his arms relaxed, his waist arched, he remained superb in his shamelessness like an antique marble.

"Who then dares," he said, "to enter without knocking?"

"I do," the baron replied furiously, "I do, my dear young scoundrel, because I want to chat with you about a few interesting things. I knew you were alone, so I crossed the threshold of the sanctuary. I'll give you a minute to make yourself decent." And he went out while Jacques, jumping out of bed, looked with trembling hands for his dressing gown.

The weather was heavy that night; it was August, and a storm was brewing. Raittolbe opened the windows of the studio and plunged his forehead into the air, which was even hotter than Jacques's bed. It was like inhaling fire. "At least it's a natural fire," he thought.

When he turned around, the young painter was waiting for him, wrapped in the long folds of an almost feminine garment; his pale face in the darkness looked like a statue's.

"Jacques," said the baron in a dull voice, "is it true that Raoule wants to marry you?"

"Yes, sir. How do you know?"

"None of your business! I know it, that's enough, I even know why you refused. It's very noble of you to have refused, M. Silvert"—and Raittolbe laughed contemptuously—"only, after that worthy attempt at dignity, you should have retired completely from Mlle de Vénérande's sun."

Jacques, ravaged by fatigue, was wondering "how come" the sun was out in his night of intoxication and what it was that this disagreeable male could want from him.

"But, Monsieur," he muttered, "what right have you?"

"Good grief!" exclaimed the baron, "the right of any man of honor, knowing what I know, when he has to deal with a scoundrel of your type. Raoule is a madwoman; her madness will go away, but if during a fit she married you, you wouldn't disappear, would you! . . .

"It would be disgusting for everyone. I've done everything possible so that our world should know nothing of this scandal, but you'll have to do the impossible for the scandal to cease altogether. The closed doors cannot last forever. Your sister could get drunk again, and then, I swear, I can't answer for the consequences. Tonight, you've behaved more or less properly. Well, what prevents you from leaving this apartment tomorrow, going to the aforementioned garret, seeking some work, and forgetting her . . . error, as it were. If you've ever had one good impulse, then everything isn't dead within you! Damn it, try to get a grip on yourself, Jacques!"

"You were listening to us," said Jacques mechanically.

"Uh! Uh! No! Someone was listening for me, in spite of me, and besides I think you've got a nerve asking me questions."

"You are Marie's lover?" Jacques went on, with an ironic smile of indulgence.

The ex-officer clenched his fists.

"If you had a drop of blood in your veins! . . . ," he growled, his eyes flashing.

"Well, baron, since I don't meddle in your affairs, don't meddle in mine," Jacques replied. "No! I won't marry Mlle de Vénérande, but I will love her wherever I please: here, elsewhere, in a drawing room, in a garret, and as I please. I take orders only from her; if I'm vile, that's my business; if she loves me that way, that's her business!"

"A thousand damnations! The thing is, that hysterical woman will end up marrying you whether you want it or not, I know her."

"Just as Marie Silvert has become your mistress whether you wanted her or not, baron, one never knows what one is capable of."

Jacques's calm and gentle tone completely changed Raittolbe. Could it be that this rent boy was telling the truth? Was beauty really no longer necessary to attain physical enjoyment? He, the elegant rake, had sunk into the mud out of devotion, and then, suddenly, the expert cynicism of the shameless guttersnipe had stabbed him in his most secret fibers, and the ferment of corruption that a moralist always carries deep within had risen to the surface. Of his own free will he had come back to Marie Silvert; he too had wanted to inspire an unhealthy passion; and this intelligent couple, Raittolbe and Raoule, had become, almost at the same time, the prey of a double bestiality.

"If only the sky would burst," shrieked the baron, shaking his fist at the storm.

Jacques went up to him.

"Is it my sister who doesn't want me to marry her?" he asked, still smiling enchantingly.

"No! damn it! quite the contrary, she wants to push you into this infernal union. Jacques! You must resist."

"Of course, Monsieur, I haven't the slightest wish for it."

"Swear to me that . . ."

The end of the sentence was cut off in the throat of the ex-officer of hussars. He could not very well extract an oath from this monster. He grabbed Jacques's arm. The latter shrank back rapidly, and as his sleeve floated off his arm, Raittolbe felt the pearly skin beneath his fingers.

"You must promise me . . ."

119

But Silvert retreated still further.

"I forbid you to touch me, Monsieur," he said coldly. "Raoule doesn't want you to."

Indignantly, Raittolbe knocked over a chair, jumped on the accursed creature whose velvet gown appeared to him now like the shadows of an abyss, and pulling off the hand rest of an easel, he struck till the stick fell to pieces.

"Now you'll find out what a real man is like, scoundrel! . . . ,"[46] howled Raittolbe, seized by a blind rage whose violence he could probably not understand and, he added, seeing Jacques crumple to the ground bruised all over:

"And she'll find out, that degenerate, that there's only one way, to my mind, to touch wretches like you! . . ."

After the baron's departure, Jacques, opening his sad eyes in the night, saw on one of the studio walls what looked like a big firefly in the middle of the draperies.

Chapter 10

So that she could see and hear what was happening in her brother's room, Marie Silvert had made a hole in the wall of her bedroom adjoining the studio.

---

[46]Raittolbe has been addressing Jacques respectfully with the *vous* form until now, but here he lapses into the *tu* form, a mark of disrespect that adds to the insult.

The firefly that Jacques saw scintillating in the dark was this hole lit up by lamplight.

Raittolbe found the prostitute in bed, drinking a cup of rum that she had just heated up on a little spirit lamp still burning beside her bed.

This room did not resemble in the least the rest of the apartment furnished with care by Raoule de Vénérande. Against striped, somewhat mildewed wallpaper stood a very heavy wardrobe of burnished mahogany with a mirror; a curtainless bed of the same mahogany, but less darkly stained; and four chairs covered with cerise chintz as if in fright around a light wood table blackened here and there by the bottom of a frying pan. To the left of the door, on the stove, where the dishes were strewn pell-mell, a certain hat spiffed up with feathers dangled one of its ribbons in a soup tureen full of melted butter.

Marie Silvert, her cheeks red, smacked her lips as she savored her rum. As she drank, she brooded tenderly over a jacket decorated with the red ribbon of the Legion of Honor, which had been thrown over the nearest of the four chairs.

"What a fool I am," mumbled Raittolbe, his arms crossed, standing beside this bed that he could not help comparing mentally with Jacques's.

"You, my fine fellow, a fool!" said Marie, scandalized.[47]

"By heaven!" the ex-officer went on, "I have just acted like a brute and not like an agent of justice."

"What have you done?" questioned the woman, letting go of her cup.

"What I did, damn it, what I did! I thrashed *Mademoiselle* your brother without even realizing it, that's how badly I have been wanting to do it for the last few weeks."

"You beat him up?"

"A major thrashing!"

"Why?"

"Ah, that's what I really don't understand. I think he insulted me, but I'm still not sure."

Marie, snuggled in her sheets, was starting to look like a contented cat.

"You were excited . . . ," she sighed. "Love often has that effect—I should have realized that you would give him a jolt! . . ."

"Let's not talk about it anymore! If Raoule complains, send her to me . . . Good evening! Obviously, I was wrong to get mixed up in your affairs. They are much too complicated for the brain of a gentleman."

---

[47]Marie and Raittolbe's use of the *tu* form alerts the reader to their intimacy.

"Are you angry with me too?" the girl asked, sitting up anxiously.

"Pah! . . ." And Raittolbe finished dressing, not wanting to say another word.

On the boulevard the fresh morning air calmed the baron down, but an almost painful obsession remained fixed in his brain, like the point of a knife in the middle of the forehead. He had struck Silvert, who did not defend himself, Silvert naked beneath his velvet robe, Silvert, his limbs already crushed from an enervating fatigue.

Why should he, the strong-minded, need to teach a lesson to a poor absurd human being? Nice work indeed! If he had only done it at once, but no! First he had become the lover of the most disgusting of prostitutes . . . He walked to the rue d'Antin, where he had a mezzanine apartment, and, entering his smoking room, locked himself in to write to Mlle de Vénérande.

Even as he began the letter, his pen slipped from his fingers. He could not in all loyalty leave her in ignorance of the cause of his brutality. On the other hand, he thought to himself, what right do I have to come between the mutual shame of these two lovers? If Raoule wanted to marry Silvert, the scandal would concern her alone; it was not his duty to guard the honor of this woman.

He had already torn up three sheets, hardly begun, when he suddenly recalled the hole pierced by Marie through the wall separating the lovers, one of whom he had just thrashed, from the rest of the world. He felt so guilty that he pushed aside all idea of accusing anybody.

He contented himself by revealing to Raoule the exact location of this opening into her private life. He confessed that, in order to *appease* Mlle Silvert's dangerous mood, he had thought it necessary to yield *to her fantasy*; that her admiration for his person reaching disquieting proportions, he intended to send her a banknote as farewell; and that he would never again set foot in the studio on the boulevard Montparnasse.

He ended by regretting the *fit of quick temper* of which Jacques had been the victim.

Raoule was to remain only a short time at the duchess d'Armonville's. She never left Paris now except for very short visits, sacrificing for her love the summer travels dictated by the fashionable world. However, the baron did not forget to note on the envelope: "Please forward." Then, his conscience at rest, he returned to his ordinary life.

Jacques was not unaware of Raoule's address, but it never occurred to him to complain. He simply took a bath and avoided any confrontations with his sister. Jacques, whose body was a poem, knew that his poem would always be read more attentively than any letter from such a vulgar writer as he. This unusual person, through contact with a beloved woman, had acquired all the feminine wiles.

In spite of his silence, Marie was astonished to see a gash on his cheek.

"It would seem that you've been bragging," she said to him tauntingly. "Did M. de Raittolbe insult you?" The girl emphasized her words with cruel irony, for in fact she thought that her brother carried a little too far his indulgence for the woman who paid.

"No! He wanted to forbid me to marry," replied Jacques bitterly.

"Well!" she grumbled, "that's not what he promised me to tell you. Ah! so that's what he wants to forbid . . . well, don't give a f[uck] about him! Your Raoule is much too stuck on you not to legalize your fun one of these days. I even advise you to push it. I have an idea."

"What is it?"

Marie planted herself on tiptoe in front of her brother.

"If you marry Mlle de Vénérande, a high-society girl, worth millions, I, your sister, might settle down as they say and become Mme la baronne de Raittolbe."

Jacques was deep in the contemplation of a little tortoiseshell box full of green paste.

"You think so! . . ."

"I am sure of it; and, God, then together we would forget the bad times, we would all belong to good society."

Jacques's eyes flashed, and his delicate complexion suddenly flushed.

"I'll be able to punish her ex-lovers when I can claim to be an honest member of society! . . ."

"Of course! But Raittolbe has never been her lover, idiot! Real women are much more to his taste, I can tell you."

"Well, then, why did he hit me so hard?" the young man objected, as a burning tear came to his eye.

Marie merely shrugged her shoulders, as though suggesting that Jacques was born to be whipped.

The next day, Raoule telegraphed that she would come the following night.

Indeed, about eight in the evening, the Vénérande mansion was all agog at Mademoiselle's unexpected return. Aunt Ermengarde, thinking that some catastrophe must have occurred, ran to meet her.

"What, darling," she cried, "you're back already! When it's so stifling here, and so nice and fresh in the country! . . ."

"Yes, my dear aunt, I'm back. Our friend the duchess's nerves are in a frightful state because the baron de Raittolbe won't go and blow the hunting horn with her. The poor baron has mysterious passions that keep him far away from us."

"Now, Raoule, don't speak ill of others," sighed the canoness, intimidated.

Raoule went to bed very early, on the pretext that she was extremely tired. At midnight, she was in a cab on her way to the left bank.

Jacques was expecting her, confident in the revenge she was bringing, for the telegram had said: "I know everything."

Without wondering how she knew everything, Jacques was counting on a terrific outburst against the one he accused of having been her happy lover.

Raoule burst impetuously into the studio, which was brilliantly lit by chandeliers and torcheres as a sign of rejoicing.

"Jaja? Where is Jaja?" she shouted, victim of a feverish impatience.

Jaja came forward, smiling with expectant lips.

She seized his hands and stopped him with a single shake.

"Tell me quickly . . . What happened? M. de Raittolbe writes me that he's sorry he discussed a very scabrous subject with you . . . those are his very words.

"You're going to give me the details, right?"

She bent over him, devouring him with her burning eyes.

"Say, what's that on your cheek . . . that big blue stripe? . . ."

"I've got plenty of others; come to our room and you'll see."

He led her away, carefully closing the portieres after them. Marie was sneering ironically, but she was uneasy; she retired to her room to put her ear to the hole in the wall.

Jacques slipped off his clothes one by one, and then Raoule uttered the cry of a she-wolf who returns to find her young slaughtered.

The idol's fine skin was striped from top to bottom with long, bluish scars.

"Ah!" the young woman cried, grinding her teeth, "they've massacred him for me!"

"A little, it's true," said Jacques, sitting on the edge of his bed to look leisurely at the new tints that his bruises were taking. "Your friend Raittolbe has a heavy fist."

"It was Raittolbe who did this to you?"

"He doesn't want me to marry you . . . he loves you, that man!"—Nothing can describe the way Jacques uttered those words.

Raoule, on her knees, was counting the brutal marks of the stick.

"I'll tear his heart out, you know? He came in here . . . ? Answer me. Don't hide anything from me!"

"I was asleep. He was coming from my sister's room. We had words about marriage . . . Then he tried to touch me to help me understand . . . I stepped back because you forbade me to let myself be touched. Do you remember? I even told him why I didn't like feeling his hand on my arm . . ."

"Enough," roared Raoule, at the height of her rage. "That man has seen you! That's enough for me, I can guess the rest. He wanted you, and you resisted him."

Jacques let out a burst of laughter:

"Are you mad, Raoule? Just because I obeyed you by forbidding him to touch me, doesn't mean that he . . . Oh, Raoule! what you dare suppose is very ugly. He struck me out of jealousy, that's all."

"Come on! My senses tell me all too plainly what a man, even a gentleman, can feel, when he finds himself face to face with Jacques Silvert . . ."

"But, Raoule . . ."

"I repeat: what I hear is enough."

She forced him to go to bed at once, went to look for a vial of arnica, and bandaged him as though he were a child in the cradle.

"You didn't look after yourself well, my dear love, you should have called a doctor!" she said when she had finished.

"I didn't want to let anyone else see me! . . . The only remedy I took was some hashish!"

Raoule remained a moment in a state of mute adoration, then she suddenly charged at him, forgetting the blue marks, overcome by a frenetic vertigo, a supreme desire to possess him through caresses just as that torturer had possessed him through blows. She squeezed him so hard that Jacques cried out in pain.

"You're hurting me!"

"All the better," she rasped. "I must erase every scar with my lips, or I'll always see you naked in front of him . . ."

"You're being unreasonable," he moaned gently, "and you're going to make me cry!"

"So cry! What does it matter, he has seen you smile!"

"Oh! You're becoming more cruel than his cruelest insult. He'll tell you himself that I was asleep . . . I couldn't have smiled at him . . . and then I put on my dressing gown!"

Jacques's naive explanations only added fuel to the fire.

"Who knows! Good God!" thought the young woman. "Maybe this creature, whom I thought was in my power, has been a depraved scoundrel for a long time."

Once the doubt had entered her mind, Raoule could control herself no longer. Violently she tore off the linen bandages she had rolled around the sacred body of her ephebe. She bit his marbled flesh, squeezed it tightly in both hands, scratched it with her pointed nails. It was a complete defloration of that marvelous beauty that, formerly, had made her swoon with a mystical happiness.

Jacques was writhing, bleeding from veritable slashes that Raoule was opening deeper with an ever more refined sadistic pleasure. All the anger of human nature that she had tried to suppress in her metamorphosed being reawoke at once, and the thirst for this blood that flowed over the twisted limbs now replaced all the pleasures of her ferocious love . . .

Immobile, her ear still stuck to the wall of her room, Marie Silvert was trying to hear what was happening; suddenly she heard a heartrending cry:

"Help! She's hurting me! Marie, help!"

She was frozen to the marrow, and since she was a *real woman*, as Raittolbe had said, she did not hesitate to run toward the slaughter . . .

Chapter 11

Every year, for the Grand Prix,[48] a reception was given at the Vénérande mansion, and in addition to the intimate circle, a few new acquaintances were always invited.

---

[48]The Grand Prix de Paris is a horse race held at Longchamp, the Paris race course that forms part of the Bois de Boulogne, at the end of June. The event traditionally marked the end of the social season; the next day the upper classes would leave Paris to spend the summer at their country estates.

This reception, less formal perhaps than the evenings when guests simply took a cup of tea, brought commoners and artists together around the canoness Ermengarde. Since Raoule had returned from the duchess d'Armonville's, a gloomy sadness never left her, as though during one of the storms that had descended on Paris recently, her brain had received a terrible jolt; and yet, as this ball drew nearer, she slowly revived from her torpor. Her aunt had clearly noticed her troubled appearance but did not seek an explanation, in the first place because her daily devotions did not require an explanation of Raoule's mood and also because she was counting on the reception in question, always very animated, to distract her *nephew*'s changeable mood.

Indeed, Mlle de Vénérande deigned to supervise and direct the preparations. She announced that the large central drawing room would be opened, as would be the room next to the conservatory, where the dazzling magnesium light would reveal the exotic flowers in all the brightness of their true nuances. Raoule could not conceive of giving a ball for the sole and monotonous pleasure of gathering together many people; she had to have the additional attraction of something original to offer her guests.

In the picture gallery, opposite the conservatory, a buffet, set up on crystal columns, would offer the sportsmen parched by the dust of Longchamp an endless fountain of Roederer champagne.

When she submitted the invitations to her aunt, Raoule said in a matter-of-fact tone:

"I'll introduce my pupil to you. You remember him? The painter of the bouquet of forget-me-nots. That young flower maker is such a courageous boy, he must be rewarded. Besides, we are to receive an architect brought by Raittolbe; it's an accepted thing now, artists are received in the best of society, otherwise we would be swamped with bourgeois who are much worse!"

"Oh! oh! Raoule," murmured Dame Ermengarde in frightened tones, "he's only a pupil, some nobody."

"But, my dear aunt, that's just why we must invite this young man. The greatest geniuses would never have succeeded if someone hadn't helped them become known."

"True; and yet . . . he struck me as coming from the lowest class, he can't have any upbringing . . ."

"Do you think my cousin René well brought up, dear aunt?"

"No, he's unbearable, even, with his backstage gossip and his theater talk, but . . . he is your cousin!"[49]

---

[49]While the theater was popular as a source of entertainment, it was considered most disreputable to be associated with the production of such entertainment. An actress was thought to be almost the same thing as a prostitute.

"Well, at least the other one doesn't belong to my family, we won't have to take responsibility for his poor upbringing, always supposing, dear aunt, that this young man really doesn't know how to behave in our society."

"Raoule, it just bothers me," the canoness repeated, "the son of a workman!"

"Who draws as if he were the son of Raphael!"

"And will he be properly dressed?"

"I'll take care of that," Mlle de Vénérande asserted with a bitter grin, and then amending her sentence so that it would not sound so enigmatic:

"He's making a good living, after all!"

"Well, I leave it to your experience, my dear Raoule," Aunt Ermengarde concluded with a heavy heart.

That same day, the baron de Raittolbe, who had not set foot in the mansion since Raoule's return, came to call. Very grave, very reserved, he gave the aunt some tickets for the private enclosure at the races without looking at her niece for so much as an instant. Raoule abandoned the new novel she was reading and held out her beautiful hand:

"Baron," she said, "our dear canoness has granted a formal invitation for your architect, you know, M. Martin Durand."

"My architect? . . . Oh, yes, of course . . . the one I met in an artistic circle, a young man with a future . . . He competed honorably at the last Universal Exposition . . .

"But Mademoiselle, I never asked . . ."

"I know you didn't insist," Raoule interrupted dryly, "but I did . . . Your friend," she stressed the word, "will be among our guests, along with M. Jacques Silvert, the painter whom we went to see together on the boulevard Montparnasse."

If the goddesses who ornamented the ceiling had crashed to the floor, Raittolbe could not have shown more surprise. This time he looked straight at Raoule, and Raoule was obliged to look back at him—two lightning bolts flew. Though he did not understand why the young woman had not answered his letter, or why Jacques was going to be "formally" one of them, the baron foresaw a catastrophe.

"I thank you on behalf of these gentlemen," he said, twirling his mustache. "Thank you; Jacques Silvert is a delightful comrade, and Martin Durand an accomplished man of the world. To open your drawing room to them, ladies, is to anticipate their future fame!"

"Well," sighed Mme Ermengarde, "you reassure me, but they have awful names, I'll have difficulty getting used to them."

They chatted for a while about the races. Raoule discussed the chances of the different stables with Raittolbe. Then, as the latter was about to leave—

"By the way, baron," Raoule cried playfully, "do you know the new Devisme pistol?"[50]

"No!"

"A masterpiece!"

"Do you have one?" answered the baron, who did not want to back down.

"Let's go to the shooting gallery," she answered, rising. "I want you to try it."

An old lady dressed in violet, with a mother-of-pearl crucifix visible above her coat, was just entering. Dame Ermengarde, delighted at not having to talk anymore about the two commoners whose names made her hair stand on end, came to greet her.

"Mme de Chailly. Ah! I'm so happy, my dear Right Honorable Lady. We have so much to talk about. Just think, Father Stéphane of Léoni is on his way; he's going to preach the autumn retreat!" She spoke with the self-important volubility of idle and pious ladies.

"All the better!" Raoule concluded, ironically, letting the portiere fall, and she disappeared, followed by the baron.

More excited than he wanted to seem, the baron maintained an absolute silence as they went down the dark passages of the mansion.

---

[50]Devisme was a French manufacturer of guns, including dueling pistols and revolvers.

The shooting gallery was a kind of vaulted terrace that Mlle de Vénérande, the true mistress of the house, had had fitted for that purpose.

Once they arrived, the baron pretended to be examining the panoplies of arms, and then—

"Where's the famous pistol?" he ventured, breaking a portentous silence.

Raoule answered by pointing to a chair; and then, very pale, but her voice not betraying her anger:

"We have to talk . . ."

"We have to talk . . . about the artists?"

"Yes, Martin Durand must vouch for Jacques Silvert. By a week from now, they must know each other. Arrange it, I don't have the time."

"Well! . . . That's what's called a very delicate mission, Raoule; if I handle it, won't I be subject to your aunt's reproaches?"

"There was a time when my aunt didn't matter to you, Raittolbe."

"Yes, but damn it, at the time you are talking about, Raoule, I was hoping to become the niece's husband!"

"Today you are her most intimate friend. Everyone accepts that you treat my aunt with the liberty of a friend of the family. And besides, you're my cousin René's mentor. These young people are about his age, introduce them . . . Do what you need to."

"At your service," Raittolbe answered, bowing.

For a moment these two friends looked at each other like two enemies before a duel.

It was obvious to Raittolbe that Raoule was hiding something; it was obvious to Raoule that Raittolbe felt guilty.

"Have you seen Jacques again?" asked the baron at last, affecting complete indifference. Mlle de Vénérande was toying with a pistol loaded only with powder, and it was with no less indifference that she took aim at the ex-officer's heart and fired. A cloud of smoke separated them.

"Very well," he said without blinking; "if you had chosen the wrong weapon, I'd be a dead man."

"Yes, since I was firing point-blank. Maybe it's a foretaste of reality; don't you think you are destined, my dear man, to die under fire?"

"Hm, as a retired officer, it's not very likely!"

In spite of his self-possession, Raittolbe found it difficult to repress a nervous trembling. Those words "under fire!" troubled him.

"I have seen Jacques again," Mlle de Vénérande went on. "He's . . . indisposed. Marie is looking after him, and I think that when he is better, this 'little yokel' will get married."

"What!" said the baron, "without your permission?"

"Mlle Silvert will marry M. Raoule de Vénérande. Does that surprise you? Why look so horrified? . . ."

"Oh! Raoule! Raoule! . . . It's impossible! it's monstrous! It's . . . it's revolting even!! You! Marry that wretch! Come on!!"

Raoule looked straight at the terrified baron with her burning eyes.

"If only to have the right to defend him from you, Monsieur!" she cried, unable to contain her lioness-like rage.

"From me!" Then, unable to hold back, Raittolbe marched up to the terrifying creature.

"Mademoiselle, when you insult me, you forget that I can't treat you like Jacques Silvert. Blood would be necessary to wipe out your words . . . What amends are you going to make?"

She smiled disdainfully:

"None, Monsieur, none! . . . Only I want you to note that you accused yourself before I thought of doing so."

"A thousand damnations!" the baron burst out, beside himself and forgetting he was in the presence of a woman. "You'll take that back."

"I said, Monsieur," retorted Raoule, "that I would defend him from you. You don't deny, I hope, having struck him?"

"No, I don't deny it at all . . . Did he tell you why?"

"You touched him . . ."

"Is that young good-for-nothing made of glass? Can't a gentleman's hand rest on his arm to emphasize affectionately some word of advice, without producing such an effect that he's ready to faint! Or am I mad, and is he the sane one?"

"I'm marrying him," repeated Mlle de Vénérande.

"Go ahead! Why should I object, after all? Marry him, Raoule, marry him."

And Raittolbe, as though broken by the shame of having been mixed up in such intrigues, fell back on his chair.

"Ah! what a pity you haven't a father or a brother," he stammered, bending the blade of a fencing sword between his fingers. The steel snapped, and one of the shards struck Raoule's wrist. Under the lace a drop of blood beaded.

"Honor is satisfied," declared Mlle de Vénérande with a hollow laugh.

"On the contrary, I am beginning to think," replied the baron brutally, "that honor has nothing to do with our actions. I quit the match, Mademoiselle," he added, "and I concede defeat to whoever takes on the dangerous mission of introducing the Antinous of the boulevard Montparnasse here."

Raoule shook her head:

"Are you afraid of doing it?"

"Be quiet . . . Instead of thinking about debasing others, take pity on yourself and on him!"

"Well, M. de Raittolbe, I still insist that you obey me!"

"Your reason?"

"I want to see you both face-to-face in my drawing room; I insist, otherwise I'll suspect you forever."

"You're worse than crazy! . . . I won't obey . . ."

Raoule held out her clasped hands, whose transparent skin was stained by some drops of blood.

"Raittolbe, the human being you hit like the meanest of animals, even though you knew him to be a coward and a weakling, I tore to pieces with my own nails. I so tortured his poor limbs, wherever your blows made a bruise, that he cried out . . . Someone came, and I, Raoule, was obliged to yield to his sister's indignation. Jacques is no more than a wound, and it's our doing; won't you help me make amends for that crime!"

The baron was deeply moved to his innermost being. Raoule was capable of anything, he knew. He did not doubt for a minute that she had worked herself up to such a state of exaltation.

"It's horrible! horrible," he muttered. "We are unworthy of humanity . . . Whether it's cowardice or love that paralyzed Jacques, we shouldn't, as thinking beings, have let ourselves get carried away like that. We ought to see him as just an irresponsible human being."

Raoule could not repress a movement of anger.

"You'll come," she said, "I want you to! But remember that I hate you and that in future I forbid you to look on him as a friend."

The baron did not pick up on this reference, which perhaps demanded yet another drop of blood.

"Does your aunt know of your marriage plans?" he asked in a calmer tone.

"No," replied Raoule. "I count on your advice in bringing her around to it. Anyway, it will happen . . . Marie Silvert demands it."

And with heartbreaking bitterness:

"I grant you the depth of my fall, but don't take advantage of my confession, M. de Raittolbe."

"Can't I do anything about the sister, Raoule? Do you want me to tip off the police?" Raittolbe added, a gentleman to the end.

"No, nothing, nothing . . . Scandal is inevitable; she is the little stone that breaks the powerful steel engine. I humiliated her, and she's taking revenge . . . Alas! I thought that for a prostitute money was everything, but now I see that, just like the daughter of the Vénérandes, she has the right to love."

"To love! Good God! You make me shudder, Raoule."

"I don't need to tell you whom, do I?"

They fell silent, their souls torn apart.

They both saw themselves prostrate on the ground, beneath the heel of an invisible enemy.

"Raoule," Raittolbe whispered gently, "if you really wanted to, we could escape from the abyss, you by never seeing Jacques again, and I by never speaking to Marie again. An hour of folly isn't one's whole life; united in our waywardness, we could also be united by our reha-bilitation. Raoule, believe me, come back to your senses . . . You're beautiful, you're a woman, you're young. Raoule, to be happy according to the laws of healthy nature, you've only to forget ever having known this Jacques Silvert; let's forget him."

Raittolbe was not thinking of Marie any longer. He had said: "Let's forget him." Raoule was somber, and gestured in fatal despair.

"I always love without resisting," she said slowly. "Whether my passion leads to heaven or hell, I don't care.

"As for you, Raittolbe, you've seen my idol too close up for me to be able to forgive you. Raittolbe, I hate you!"

"Good-bye, Raoule," said the baron, holding out his open hand to her. "Good-bye! I pity you."

She did not move. So he clasped her wrist and shook it with sincere affection. But as he left the fencing room and was putting on his gloves, he saw on his fingers a slight trace of blood.

He recalled at once the incident of the broken sword; and yet a superstitious terror seized him; the officer of hussars could not repress a shiver.

Chapter 12

Martin Durand was an easygoing sort of boy whose only desire was to get on in the world and in every possible sort of society. After an hour's chat with Jacques Silvert, he had taken him under his protection and was on a first-name basis with him. In his view, only a pair of compasses could take one far. Flowers, however marvelously done, had only the value of useless baubles, for which the artist might be paid a very high price once and then be ruined by their accumulation. Palaces are built all year round, but flowers are only occasionally in demand.

"Take for example," he cried, "the heaps of roses, the carts of violets, the piles of tulips that ornament your walls. My dear fellow, too many flowers! I feel suffocated just looking at them!"

Thereupon he lit a cigar to offset the imaginary smell of the painted bouquets.

Jacques, who had fallen as taciturn as all who carry in their hearts the weight of great shame, answered Martin Durand's tirades only in monosyllables, and when the latter, amazed by the luxury of the studio, asked if his uncle was a millionaire, he felt himself tremble before this new friend, as he would have trembled before a new torturer.

"At last," cried Martin Durand, a real lad of the people, full of exuberance and proud of having reached his position by shoving others aside, "we're going to launch ourselves at the same time, my dear fellow! Raittolbe swears it.

"A noble drawing room, millionaire amateurs, and pretty women . . . My head is spinning! By Jove! Mme de Vénérande has the most beautiful mansion in the whole of Paris. Renaissance style, with arched windows and Louis XV iron balconies. I don't know whether she pays a lot for your studies of forget-me-nots; but the devil take me if she doesn't give me an order to pull down a pavilion and rebuild it as a tower for her. We'll help each other . . . You'll tell her that I'm the architect who's all the rage. And I'll let her know that the president of the republic has ordered a bunch of peonies from you."

Jacques smiled painfully. This expansive fellow was happy, he earned his living by fighting with stone; he was strong, he was honest, and after all his sallies, he would sigh about his beautiful cousin, the daughter of the director of one of the biggest stores in the capital. Nobility, love, money, everything would flow his way, at a sign from him, because he was a man.

On the basis of this extensive familiarity, Martin Durand declared that he would call for Jacques on the day of the ball, and on seeing again his friend Raittolbe whom he knew at least as well as his friend Silvert, he said to him in delighted tones:

"That boy is the most superb type of professional model I've ever met; of course he doesn't have the slightest trace of talent . . . But I'll make something of him."

Artists are generally afflicted with the monomania of wishing that good society should admire not their merit but their bad manners: they especially insist on attracting disciples when they want to teach what they know nothing about.

Martin Durand stroked his brown beard and added:

"Yes, I'll make something of him. He's twenty-three; he can change. I think I'll really astonish him at the Vénérandes', even if the patents of nobility of all these people were in Egyptian granite."

Could one still astonish Jacques Silvert? Raittolbe did not answer.

The evening of the Grand Prix, at about ten, the center drawing room and the conservatory with the exotic plants were flooded by dazzling jets of magnesium, a fluid white light, clearer and yet less blinding than electricity. Under its glare all the relief of the statues, all the folds of draperies stood out, as if daylight itself wished to take part in the reception at the Vénérandes.

The forefathers in doublets, the foremothers in Medici ruffs, from their high frames, with swords or fans, seemed to point out to each other the specimens of Parisian common folk they saw parading past their feet.

The sporting reception had indeed mixed everybody up, those who descended from Adam and those who descended from the Crusades. The architect Martin Durand and the duchess d'Armonville, Mme Ermengarde the canoness and Jacques Silvert, the rent boy. With the marvelous understanding of people who want to amuse themselves, each according to his lights, at the expense of others, they all exchanged the most gracious welcoming smiles. Standing close to her aunt's monumental armchair, Mlle de Vénérande was receiving with a rather haughty grace that owed more to a gentleman of olden times than to a simply coquettish woman.

When the strange creature abandoned passion's domain and stopped running ahead of her century, she went right back to the era when the chatelaine of the castle refused to lower the drawbridge for badly dressed troubadours.

That evening Raoule wore a very filmy white gauze dress with a court train. She had not a single jewel, not a single flower. A bizarre whim had made her tie on her exposed shoulders a cuirass of gold mail, so finely meshed that her bust appeared to be molded in liquid gold.

To demarcate the flesh from the cloth, a cord of diamonds coiled around her neck, and in her black hair, piled up like a Greek helmet, she had pinned a diamond crescent, with phosphorescent points like moonbeams. The superb Diana seemed to walk on a cloud. Her head, with its pure profile, dominated the company, and it was not without a certain anxious admiration that anyone dared meet her sparkling eyes. The canoness was prudishly swathed in a shroud of lace that covered a dark violet dress. Her small, gentle face, parchment-like, with eyes the color of a pale-blue sky, took refuge under the coat of arms emblazoned on her armchair, which in contrast seemed ready to crack under the powerful pressure of Raoule's arm.

On their right a group formed around Cousin René, a rare specimen of the top-notch sportsman, explaining to whoever wanted to listen how *Sinbad the Sailor* had won by a length and why the gold silk was worn beautifully that year . . . Raittolbe, severe, his Slavic mask inscrutable, thought of the ancient Gorgon when he looked at Mlle de Vénérande. Then there was the old marquis de Sauvarès, hopping about like a big night bird blinded by the crude light, all the while coveting with his dull eyes, enlivened sometimes by a flash of lubricity, the round shoulders of his goddaughter Raoule.

148

Around them a swarm of exquisitely gowned women were entertaining one another, with a persistence that annoyed the men, about the exploits of John Mare, the winning jockey.

In the crowd the amateur artists could be recognized by their constant flux, forming a tide near the tulle or lace trains, the aim of their movements being to approach one famous star or another.

As for the real artists, they were working the same course, but in the opposite direction, so that the drawing room was transformed at times into another racetrack, of a very discreet kind. During one of these fluctuations, Raoule, whose eyes took in everything, made a sign to Raittolbe. He started, then looked in the direction indicated by the young woman's barely raised finger. He was there, and Martin Durand was shoving him violently.

"Go on! stupid, go on! . . . ," he was grumbling, "you'll have to start talking to her somehow, while I study this bust. Damn nobility! . . . Only they can carve you such caryatids. What a curve, lads! What a bosom, what shoulders, what arms! I can see her now holding up the balcony of the restored Louvre.[51] How she freezes your

---

[51]The Louvre Palace, formerly a royal residence in Paris, became a museum in 1791. It was extended by Napoleon III under the Second Empire, the regime that had just ended in 1870.

blood just by the way she stands on one hip. Go on, I'm right behind you . . ."

Jacques refused to move forward; bewildered by the floods of magic brightness in this magnificent drawing room, treading on the dresses spread out all around, intoxicated by the heady scents emanating from the coiffures powdered with jewels, the ex-working-class flower maker felt as though he were still the prey of the heavenly vertigo afforded him by the fumes of the hashish.

"What a ninny, my poor little painter!" Martin Durand was saying, very annoyed at having to witness this want of audacity in a comrade. "By Jove, show a little more self-confidence! Stare down the women, jostle the men, here, copy me . . . Are two lads like us afraid of the footlights? Ah, there's M. de Raittolbe! We'll be all right now."

As a matter of fact, the architect hardly had a better head on his shoulders than the painter, but he had the inimitable self-assurance of all wreckers who know a little bit about rebuilding.

The baron de Raittolbe shook his hand, but avoided touching his friend's.

"Gentlemen, delighted to see you. I'll take charge of introducing you . . ." And he led them straight up to Raoule.

"Mademoiselle," he said, loudly enough to be heard by the main group of guests, "let me introduce to you

M. Martin Durand, architect, to whom the capital is indebted for a few more beautiful monuments, and M. Jacques Silvert."

The result of this brief introduction was that no one bothered at all about the monument person, since everyone knew right away what he was capable of. Monocles were instead aimed at the one who had only an unknown name. Jacques remained rooted, looking into the eyes of Raoule, whom he had not seen since the sinister night.

He started like a man who wakes with a jump.

His flesh quivered; he became once more the body tamed by that infernal mind who appeared to him there, clothed in gold armor like a symbolic shield.

He remembered suddenly that in her presence he was complete, that he became her joy once again, just as she was his suffering. His initial intoxication vanished, to be replaced by the servile love of the grateful animal. His wounds closed at the memory of her caresses. An expression at once happy and resigned made his beautiful mouth smile. Without thinking that people were looking at him, Jacques murmured:

"God, why did you make me come here? I'm nothing, and you don't even think me worthy of martyrdom anymore!"

A vague flush rose to Raoule's temples, and she stammered:

"But, Monsieur, you must believe that through her admiration for your work, my aunt concluded that you were very . . ."

"Thank you, Madame," added Jacques, turning to the canoness, who was stunned to see him so elegant in his ballroom clothes; "thank you, but I'm sorry that you are kinder than Mlle Raoule!"

"That's perfectly natural!" stuttered the saint, completely missing his point and accustomed in her world to answer without hearing.

Only Raittolbe, the marquis de Sauvarès, Cousin René, and Martin Durand pricked up a worried ear.

"Kinder than Mlle Raoule! . . . What?" said René with a satisfied grin. "He's rather vulgar, this Jacques Silvert. Kinder . . . don't get it! . . ."

"Neither do I," grumbled the old marquis. "Something fishy! . . . perhaps! Ha! ha! . . . An Adonis, upon my word, an Adonis!"

Martin Durand was pulling at his pretty beard.

"I'm sunk!" he thought. "The boy's quite gone on her, and they all seem to be trying to one-up each other. What curves, what a caryatid, lads!"

Raittolbe, astonished by the sudden self-assurance of this depraved lowlife, nevertheless admitted to himself it almost reconciled him to Jacques. Some women moved closer to Jacques. The duchess d'Armonville, contemplating the marvelous features of this redhead whom the starry whiteness of the lighting rendered as blond as a Titian Venus, helped the hesitant ones decide with a boyish exclamation that suited her perfectly, as she had short and curly hair:

"By Jove, ladies, I'm amazed!"

Just then the orchestra, hidden in a stand overlooking the room, let out the prelude to a waltz from the friezes above. Couples shook into action, and Raoule, taking advantage of the stir, moved away from her aunt, followed by a small court. Jacques leaned over to her.

"You're very beautiful . . . ," he whispered ironically, "but I'm sure your dress will get in your way when you dance!"[52]

"Hush, Jacques!" begged Mlle de Vénérande, dismayed. "Hush! I thought I'd taught you to play your role as a man of the world differently!"

"I'm not a man! I'm not of the world!" replied Jacques, quivering with powerless rage. "I'm the beaten animal who comes back to lick your hands! I'm the slave who loves while serving as an amusement! You taught me to speak so that I could say *here* that I belong to you! . . . No

---

[52]Jacques has been using the polite *vous* form with Raoule, as befitting his station in life so far as the public knows it, but here they slip into the *tu* form, an inappropriate display of intimacy in this public setting, hence Raittolbe's warning.

use marrying me, Raoule; one doesn't marry one's mistress; that's not done in your drawing rooms! . . ."

"Oh! You're frightening me! . . . Now, Jacques! Is this how you avenge yourself! Is Marie dead? Is our love no longer cursed? Haven't I seen your blood? Is it possible to relive the madness of our happiness? No! Don't say any more! Your breath, perfumed with young love, makes me feverish! . . ."

Raittolbe, nearest to them, whispered:

"Be careful, you're being watched! . . ."

"Then let's waltz!" said Raoule, suddenly carried away by the savagery of her sensual desire, which had returned in greater force in the presence of the tempter.

Jacques, without any of the usual polite formalities, clasped Raoule, who bent like a reed under his embrace, and the circle opened.

"It's an abduction!" said the marquis de Sauvarès. "This Jacques Silvert tackles our goddess as if she were an ordinary mortal! . . ."

"The caryatid has grown feet!" sighed Martin Durand, distressed at having witnessed such a profane metamorphosis.

René was trying to laugh:

"Amusing! Very amusing! Exceedingly funny. My cousin tames him all the better to devour him! Yet another one . . . When we get to a hundred, we'll make a notch! Very amusing! . . ."

Raittolbe watched them waltz with a dreamy look. This yokel waltzed well, and his supple body, with its feminine undulations, seemed made for this graceful exercise. He did not try to hold his partner, but made himself part of her, one waist, one torso, one being. To see them pressed together turning round and round and melting in an embrace where their flesh, despite their clothes, molded together, one could picture the single divinity of love in two people, that *complete* individual spoken of in the fabulous tales of Brahmins, two distinct sexes in one unique monster.[53]

---

[53]Rachilde may have been thinking of the myth in Plato's *Symposium*, that human beings were originally made up of two beings joined together. There were three sexes: male-male, female-female, and male-female (hermaphrodite). Zeus punished human beings by cutting them in two, but as a result each half has sought ever since to be reunited with its original other half; thus Plato's myth acts as a kind of just-so story that explains sexual desire and accounts for the existence of both heterosexual and homosexual forms of attraction. It is also in the *Symposium* that Plato describes two Venuses, the celestial and the terrestrial, thus defining that double identity of Venus that will become so important in the nineteenth century. In the conversion of Plato's homoerotic philosophy to Christian morality, the celestial Venus becomes the goddess of licit and conjugal love, while the terrestrial aspect becomes the goddess of lust and carnal desire. Writing about the Salon of 1863, Maxime du Camp, for example, offered a history of the figure of Venus that attempted to account for the transformation of Plato's original monster, which embodied both male and female attributes into the goddess of female beauty.

"Yes, the flesh!" he thought. "Healthy flesh, the sovereign power of the world! She's right, that perverted creature! Jacques could have all the nobility, all the knowledge, all the talent, all the courage, but if his complexion were not as lovely as a rose, we wouldn't stare at him with such wonder in our eyes!"

"Jacques!" Raoule was saying, yielding to the intoxication of a bacchante . . . "Jacques, I'm marrying you, not because I'm concerned about your sister's threats but because I want you in the open light of day, after having had you during our mysterious nights. You'll be my beloved wife just as you've been my beloved mistress!"

"And then you'll reproach me with having sold myself, right?"

"Never!"

"You know that I'm not quite healed yet! . . . that I'm an *ugly girl*! What good am I to you! . . . Jaja's ruined! . . . Jaja looks awful!" he went on in cajoling tones, pressing her more tightly.

"I swear I'll make you forget everything! It would be so nice to be your husband! to call you privately Mme de Vénérande! . . . because it's my name I'm giving you!"

According to Jennifer Shaw, it is this version of Venus in the nineteenth century that turns the hermaphrodite (embodying both male and female attributes) into two single-sexed people: a woman who depends on the male creative artist for her power. For more on du Camp and the Salon of 1863, see Shaw.

"That's true! I haven't got a name of my own! . . ."

"Come on, your sister is our providence! She forced me to make a promise I won't retract . . . My angel! my god! my favorite illusion!"

When they stopped, they thought they were in the studio in the boulevard Montparnasse, and they smiled, exchanging a last vow.

"Do you know that the lion of the evening is M. Jacques Silvert?" declared Sauvarès to a group of surrounding scandalized sportsmen.

"Where does this Antinous come from?" asked the rakes, curious to pick up some shady story at the expense of the new favorite.

"He comes at Mlle de Vénérande's pleasure," replied the marquis, and his witty remark soon enjoyed a great success.

But suddenly Jacques's arrival, carelessly disturbing them in their disdainful reflections, reduced them to silence. They were about to move off en masse to show their contempt for this obscure dauber of forget-me-nots when they all felt at the same time a bizarre commotion that riveted them to the spot. Jacques, his head thrown back, still had his smile of a young girl in love; his open lips showed off his pearly teeth; his eyes, enhanced by bluish circles, maintained a glistening radiance; and under his thick hair, his delicate ears, opening like some purple flower, made all of them shiver inexplicably at once. Jacques passed them without noticing them; his hips, well defined under his evening clothes, brushed them lightly for a second . . . and with one movement they clenched their hands, suddenly grown moist.

When he had moved far off, the marquis let fall this banal phrase:

"It's very hot in here, gentlemen; 'pon my honor, it's unbearable! . . ."

They all repeated in chorus:

"It's unbearable! . . . 'Pon our honor, it's too hot! . . ."

Chapter 13

"Come on! *en garde!* one, two! Wrong, wrong, let's start over! Keep your knees bent! Some spring! Your hand at the height of your right nipple, the point at eye level. Cover yourself, thrust with the sword, one, two, lunge . . .

"Jeez! . . . Limp as a rag! Ah! my boy, you're a dazzling swordsman, but only if you don't attack or counter! By thunder! Doesn't it fire you up to feel that?"

And furiously Raittolbe made his sword grind on Jacques's.

"You're in too much of a hurry, baron!" protested Raoule, who was sitting in on the lesson, in a fencing costume. "It's not so bad now. Rest, Jacques, rest!"

Raoule took the foil from his hands, came and stood in front of Raittolbe, fell *en garde,* and vigorously delivered three thrusts that a fencing master would have been proud of.

"Hit, hit, hit!" cried the ex-officer three times one after the other, taken off guard less by the impetuosity of the charge than by the overflowing anger that it stemmed from. He had already seen Raoule's eyes light up the same way the day he left this very room with blood on his finger.

Just then Cousin René entered with several intimates. A servant who followed announced lunch, then went up to Jacques and whispered something discreetly in his ear, while the new arrivals formed a circle around the two champions, judging the blows, and naturally they could not stop talking about Mlle de Vénérande's exceptional performance. Raoule, totally absorbed in her furor, did not see Jacques slip into the adjacent smoking room.

Jacques had finally obtained from the canoness Ermengarde the right of free access to the house; he had been officially engaged to Raoule for a month. After the Grand Prix ball, at which all the scandal lovers had been shocked by the introduction of this young Silvert, Raoule, as crazy as the possessed women of the Middle Ages who had devils inside them and were no longer responsible for their actions, one morning brutally declared herself beside the bed of the unhappy canoness. It had been a very cold, very

159

dark, very gray morning. The canoness, under her emblazoned blankets, was dreaming of hair shirts and frozen paving stones. She was awakened by the sonorous voice of her *nephew* ordering her maid to make a roaring fire.

"Why a fire? Today's my day of mortification, my dear child," said the aunt, opening her eyelids, as transparent and as pale as consecrated wafers.

"Because, my dear aunt, I've come to talk over with you some very serious matters, and these serious matters will be such a natural mortification that they'll be more than enough!"

With a nasty laugh, the young woman sat down in an armchair, covering her chilly feet with her ermine-lined dressing gown.

"At this time of day? Heavens, you awoke very bright and early, my darling! Well, I'm listening." And the canoness propped herself up on her pillow, her eyes large with fright.

"Aunt Ermengarde, I want to get married!"

"Get married! Oh, Saint Philippe de Gonzague must have inspired you, for I pray to him about that every vigil.[54] Get married! Raoule! But then I'll be able to fulfill

---

[54]Although a Saint Philippe de Gonzague does not appear in lists of persons canonized or beatified by the Catholic Church, the life of Saint Aloysius Gonzaga (1568–91), beatified in 1605 and canonized in 1726, is germane in this context. Aunt Ermengarde feels responsible for Raoule's spiritual education, and for this reason it is important to

my dearest wish, to leave this world of vanities and retire to the Visitandines, where my veil is waiting for me. Blessed be the Lord!

"Of course," she added, "the baron de Raittolbe is the bridegroom-elect?" And she smiled a little mischievously.

"No, it's not Raittolbe, Aunt! I warn you I have no desire to be ennobled any further. Awful names please me much more than all the titles on our useless family parchments. I want to marry the painter Jacques Silvert!"

The canoness jerked upright in her bed, raised her virginal arms above her chaste head, and cried:

"The painter Jacques Silvert? Did I hear correctly? That fop, homeless and penniless, to whom you give charity? . . ."

For a moment astonishment paralyzed her tongue; then she went on, falling back on her pillows:

"You'll make me die of shame, Raoule!"

"My aunt," the indomitable daughter of the Vénérandes said, "the shame might be in my not marrying him!"

"Do explain what you mean!" groaned Madame Ermengarde in despair.

"Out of respect for you, my aunt, don't make me. You've loved in too saintly a way to . . ."

---

know that Benedict XIII declared Saint Aloysius Gonzaga the special protector of young students and that Pius XI proclaimed him patron of Christian youth. (We are grateful to Brody Smith for helping us identify this reference.)

"I represent your mother, Raoule . . ." interrupted the canoness with great dignity. "It's my duty to hear everything."

"Well then, I'm his mistress!" answered Raoule, with terrifying calm.

Her aunt turned as pale as the immaculate sheets around her. In the depths of her uncertain eyes flashed the only bolt of anger of her pious existence, and she said in a hollow voice:

"May the will of God be done . . . Make your mésalliance, my niece. I have enough tears left to wash away your crime . . . I'll enter the convent the day after your wedding! . . ."

And from that cold morning on, when an infernal fire had burned in the fireplace of the canoness, who yet remained mortified to the marrow, Raoule did as she liked. Her fiancé was presented to her family and her intimates; and then, without any objection being raised against this capricious fantasy, each had bowed ceremoniously to Jacques. The marquis de Sauvarès had declared he was "not bad." René, the cousin, thought him "amusing, exceedingly amusing!" The duchess d'Armonville had laughed enigmatically, and, on the whole, since a distant uncle had died at the right moment and left the magnificent dauber a fortune of three hundred thousand francs, he became a little less ridiculous.

This fortune had come straight from Raoule into the hands of the man of her choice.

The servants in the mansion said, belowstairs: he's a foundling.

A foundling to place a bar of mourning on the bright escutcheon of the Vénérandes!

Often during the sad autumnal nights, the sound of drawn-out sobs could be heard from the direction of Mme Ermengarde's closed bedroom; it could almost be mistaken for the wind whistling through the stark courtyard of the main entrance . . .

Raoule was still fencing. Raittolbe was obliged to break off. Then suddenly they heard a short interjection, sharp and discordant. They both stopped at once. They had recognized Marie Silvert's voice.

Mlle de Vénérande, under the pretext of being a little tired and without thinking of the baron or her admirers, walked toward the smoking-room door. Raittolbe did likewise.

"Seconds," said Raoule decisively, "go to the reconciliation lunch. We'll tidy up and follow you in a few minutes."

These gentlemen went out, discussing the blows exchanged.

"What have you come here for?" Jacques was saying behind the boudoir door. "To make a scene?"

"I'm not that stupid. They'd have me locked up!"

"Well, then!" said Jacques impatiently, "keep quiet."

"Yes, my boy, of course, I'm going to keep quiet, count on it. Ah! the gentleman's going to become an honest man. Mlle de Vénérande's going to marry him. What was I thinking? No more joking around! Just think! Well, on the contrary, my boy, there's going to be some joking around, and in a way that you aren't going to find quite so funny, what's more!"

"What are you driving at?"

"What am I driving at? I want you to tell your Raoule that her conditions are not mine. I couldn't care less about that scrap of paper she sent me. So, my lovebirds, it seems I'm in the way. We're ashamed of Marie Silvert, we have to get rid of her, like a tramp, send her to the country, to some corner, for a few cents she'll be only too happy to leave you alone. Well, I'm not gonna go! We've starved together, and now that you're going to feast on roast, I want my fair share of it, or else I'll upset the applecart. Yes! Monsieur's gonna swan around in his carriage from morning till night, he's such a dear heart, they dress him up like a little miss, nothing's too good for him! And his sister's gotta wear rags, use scraps for hats, eat crusts. You gotta be kidding! You thought your six-hundred-franc pension would zip my mouth, nice try, but I won't let myself be fooled; Marie Silvert doesn't go for that kind of bread, there's not enough butter on it."

"Don't give it another thought," said Mlle de Vénérande, as she entered just then, followed by Raittolbe. "Don't torment yourself, you're getting nothing!"

Raoule spoke coldly, letting her words fall one by one, and for a moment they appeared to have the effect of a cold shower on the girl.

"Fine," she said, biting her lips and sorry at not being able to get back to the subject of the six hundred francs by gentle means, "fine"; and then, digging her fingers into the back of a chair:

"In fact, I prefer it, because you disgust me—not you, sir," she said, trying to smile at Raittolbe, who was sheltering behind Raoule, whom he regretted having followed; "and yet you're the one who caused it all."

"What!" said Raittolbe, coming forward. "What are you saying?"

"It's clear: you know that Mademoiselle and Monsieur have never forgiven me for having been your mistress. It rubbed them the wrong way!"

"That's enough," the baron interrupted roughly; "don't use our affair as a pretext to go on with your insults. You did your job, I paid you: we're even."

"That's true," answered Marie, suddenly calm. "I even have here the hundred francs you sent me; I still haven't touched them. It did something to me when I got them. It may be idiotic, but that's how it is."

She spoke thus with great submission, looking at Raittolbe with almost beseeching eyes.

"You see, sir," she went on, without paying any more attention to her brother and Raoule, "being a poor working girl doesn't mean a person doesn't have a heart. You say that I just did my job with you, but you know that's not true! I loved you, I still love you, and you've only to say the word if you like, I'd do anything for . . ."

"I'm not asking any such thing of you!" interrupted Raittolbe, who felt ridiculous in Raoule's eyes, and, especially infuriating, ridiculous in Jacques's eyes. "I'll be satisfied to see you go."

Genuinely moved a moment before, the girl now felt her anger rising again. She saw Raoule and Jacques exchange a meaningful smile while glancing at her, so she burst out:

"All right! I'll go, but I have to get it off my chest! You can shrug all you want, you lot, but I'm not through, this is the last straw. You think it's amusing, don't you?

"It's funny," she jeered hideously. "You're pleased, aren't you? You were annoyed because I caught his eye, and now he's dumping me. D[amn] it, what a funny lot, are they the only ones who can have a laugh? Think again! Since I can't find one man who'll have me, I'm gonna have them all—it's gonna be a real honor for you, kids, and now I have the honor of announcing my entry into a b[rothel]."

"That won't change your way of life much," jeered Mlle de Vénérande, going toward the door and signaling to Jacques to follow her.

Jacques remained planted in front of his sister, his fists clenched, his face pale, biting his lips; perhaps there was only one dishonor for which he had not been prepared in his bumpy fall . . .

"Bon voyage!" Raoule said ironically, on the threshold of the fencing room.

"Oh! we'll see each other again, sister-in-law," replied Marie, sneering. "On my days off I'll come to pay my respects.

"You won't be able to pretend you're disgusted, you know; Marie Silvert, even with a yellow ticket, will be just as good as Mme Silvert; at least she makes love like everyone else, she does!"

She didn't finish. Jacques, beside himself and before Raittolbe could stop him, seized his sister by the wrist and shook her desperately with terrible effect.

"Will you shut up, you wretch?" he growled in a hollow voice like a death rattle. Then his muscles relaxed, and Marie, spinning around, rolled to the floor at his feet.

Marie picked herself up, went to the door, opened it, and then, turning to her brother, on each side of whom stood Raittolbe and Raoule like two bodyguards, said:

"You shouldn't wear yourself out like that, my boy. You need your strength, you need enough for two . . . and look! you're losing it already. You look like the day you were done over. You know, the doing over the baron gave you. Watch out, you're going to faint, you've got something wrong with you, of course: your chaste spouse won't get her heart's content . . .

"Doesn't he look pretty like that, between his two men!"

Marie let fly those last words with a ferocious laugh, the bursts of which must have shaken the Vénérandes' old mansion to its foundations.

Marie Silvert and Dame Ermengarde, the good angel who had tolerated and the demon of abjection who had excited, were both fleeing at the same time—one to Paradise, the other to the abyss—that monstrous love, which, in its pride reached higher than heaven, and in its depravity fell lower than hell.

Chapter 14

About midnight, the guests at Jacques Silvert's wedding noticed something very strange: the young bride was still among them, but the young bridegroom had disappeared. A sudden indisposition, a lover's quarrel, a serious accident, all possible conjectures were entertained by the clan of intimates, already completely engrossed by this union. The marquis de Sauvarès suggested that Jacques had found a challenge from an unhappy rival under his napkin, at the beginning of the marvelous meal that had been served to them. René maintained that Aunt Ermengarde was to leave society that very night and that she was transferring her powers to the husband. Martin Durand, the bridegroom's witness, was grumbling openly, because artists always have a right to *go at it* when someone needs them. He could not bear that Jacques now. In a corner of the monumental fireplace, where the husband's new hearth was collapsing into red embers,[55] the duchess d'Armonville, pensive, holding her eyeglasses between her tapering fingers, was watching Raoule, who stood opposite. Raoule was mechanically shredding her orange-blossom bouquet. Raittolbe was assuring the duchess in an undertone that love was the only power capable of really smoothing out the political difficulties of the government of the moment.

---

[55]The French word *foyer* means literally a hearth or fireplace, but it is commonly used metonymically to refer to a household. Thanks to this double meaning, the image of the collapsing red embers clearly prefigures the bloody red end of Jacques's union with Raoule.

169

"Yes but," the duchess murmured, not paying the slightest attention to the inanities of the baron, "can you tell me why our dear bride had her hair done today in such an . . . unusual fashion? It's been worrying me ever since the wedding ceremony."

"No doubt marriage, for Mme Silvert, is only another way of taking the veil," replied Raittolbe, hiding a sardonic smile.

Mme Silvert was wearing a long dress of silver brocade and a sort of swansdown jacket. Her veil had been removed at the beginning of the ball, and the wreath of orange blossoms was resting on her tight curls like a tiara on a boy's head. Her bold face harmonized admirably with these short curls but in no way resembled that of a modest bride ready to lower her eyes beneath her perfumed tresses, which the impatience of the bridegroom would soon unpin.

"I tell you," the duchess reiterated, "Raoule's had her hair cut off."

"A recent fashion that I'm adopting permanently, my dear duchess," answered Raoule, who had just overheard and was emerging from her reverie.

Raittolbe applauded silently. He tapped the palm of his hand with the tip of his fingers. Mme d'Armonville bit her lips to keep from laughing. Poor Raoule, if she went on growing more masculine, would end up compromising her husband!

The bridesmaids came forward noisily in a tumult to serve some cake according to the new custom imported from Russia that was all the rage in high society that year. Still the bridegroom did not appear. Raoule had to keep her helping of the cake intact. Midnight struck; so the young woman crossed the immense drawing room proudly and haughtily. As she reached the triumphal arch made from all the plants in the conservatory, she turned around and gave those assembled the wave of a queen dismissing her subjects. With a gracious but brief remark, she thanked her guests, then she backed out, saluting them with the elegant and rapid gesture of a swordsman's salute. The doors closed once more.

In the left wing, at the far end of the mansion, was the bridal chamber. The wing in which she found herself was at an angle to the rest of the building. The deepest darkness and the most discreet silence reigned in this part of the house.

The passages were lit by lanterns of blue Bohemian glass with the gas turned down low, and in the library next to the bedroom a single candelabrum held by a bronze slave served as a beacon. Just as Raoule entered its circle of light in the center of the room, a woman

171

dressed as simply as a servant emerged from the heavy draperies.

"What do you want?" murmured the bride, drawing herself up and letting the immense train of her silver dress trail around her feet.

"To say good-bye to you, my niece,"[56] replied Mme Ermengarde, whose pale face, suddenly illuminated, seemed to surge forward like a spectral evocation.

"You! Aunt, are you leaving?"

Moved, Raoule held out her arms.

"Won't you kiss your *nephew* one last time?" she said, in a more respectful and sweet voice.

"No!" said the canoness, shaking her head. "In heaven perhaps! But here I cannot bring myself to condone with my forgiveness the defilements of a fallen woman. Good-bye, Mlle de Vénérande. But before my departure I want you to know: however holy God wishes me to be, he has allowed me to learn of your horrible excesses. I know everything: Raoule de Vénérande, I curse you."

The canoness spoke in a very low tone, and yet Raoule seemed to hear the echoes of that curse resound all the way to the quiet of the nuptial chamber.

---

[56]Ermengarde now addresses Raoule in the formal and distancing *vous* form.

She shivered superstitiously.

"You know everything? Explain your words, Aunt! Has the sorrow of seeing me take a commoner's name made you lose your reason?"

"You're the sister-in-law of a prostitute. She was here a short while ago, this girl, although you had forgotten to invite her; she forced me to look into the abyss. You weren't Jacques Silvert's mistress, Raoule de Vénérande, and I regret it now with all my soul! But remember, Daughter of Satan, that abnormal desires are never satisfied! You'll meet despair just when you believe in happiness! God shall plunge you into doubt when you think you have reached security. Good-bye . . . I'm going to pray under another roof."

Raoule, paralyzed by the powerlessness of her rage, let her depart without uttering a word.

When Mme Ermengarde had disappeared, the bride called her maids, who were waiting to help her get ready for bed.

"Did someone come to see my aunt?" she questioned, in a husky voice.

"Yes, Madame," answered Jeanne, one of her chambermaids, "a heavily veiled person who talked to her for a long time."

"And that person?"

"Went away carrying a small box. I think that Madame the canoness made one final charitable gift before leaving for her convent."

"Ah! very well; a final charitable gift."

Just then the noise of a carriage lightly rattled the panes of the library.

"Your aunt has ordered the carriage," said Jeanne, bowing her head so as not to show her emotion.

Raoule went to the dressing room and, pushing her away, said:

"I don't want anyone; go away and have someone tell the marquis de Sauvarès, my godfather, that henceforth he'll be alone as host."

"Yes, Madame."

Jeanne went out at once, completely bewildered. The air in the Vénérande mansion seemed to have become unbreathable.

One by one the guests filed past the marquis, who was even more stunned than they by the order he had just received. When only Raittolbe was left, M. de Sauvarès took him by the arm.

"Let's be off, my dear fellow," he said, with a mocking laugh. "This house has decidedly turned into a tomb."

The footman in charge of the hall turned off the lights, and soon, in the deserted reception rooms, in the whole mansion, along with the silence there reigned the deepest darkness.

After she had bolted the door of her dressing room, Raoule divested herself of her clothes with proud anger.

"At last!" she said, when the brocade dress with chaste highlights had fallen at her impatient feet. She took a small copper key, opened a closet hidden among the draperies, and took out a black evening suit, complete from the patent leather boots to the embroidered formal shirt. In front of the mirror, which returned to her the image of a man as handsome as all the heroes of novels girls dream about, she slid her hand, with the shining wedding ring, through her short curly hair. A bitter smile played on her lips, blurred by an imperceptible brownish down.

"Dear Aunt," she said coldly, "happiness becomes more real the more it's insane. If Jacques doesn't waken from the sensual sleep that I've insinuated in his obedient limbs, I'll be happy despite your curse."

She went to a velvet portiere, raised it with a feverish gesture, and stopped, her breast heaving.

From the threshold it looked like a scene from a fairy tale. From that pagan sanctuary erected in the midst of modern splendor emanated a subtle, incomprehensible dizziness that would have galvanized any human nature. Raoule was right . . . love can be born in any cradle prepared for it.

Mlle de Vénérande's former bedroom, rounded at the corners, with a ceiling shaped like a cupola, was covered with blue velvet and paneled with white satin with gold accents and marble fluting.

A carpet designed by Raoule covered the parquet floor with all the beauties of oriental flora. Woven from thick wool, this carpet had such vivid colors and such striking relief that it was like walking on some enchanted flower bed.

In the center, under the night-light held by four silver chains, the nuptial bed had the shape of the primitive vessel that bore Venus to Cythera.[57] A swarm

---

[57]A Greek island in the Aegean where Venus had a temple. After arriving on earth, the goddess was carried there on a seashell (echoed in the form of Raoule's bed), an image perhaps familiar to many from Sandro Botticelli's painting of the birth of Venus (c.1485). In addition to this iconic representation, the theme was treated more recently in several paintings of 1863 that were exhibited in the Salon of that year, including Eugène-Emmanuel Amaury-Duval's *The Birth of Venus*, Paul Baudry's *The Pearl and the Wave*, and Alexandre Cabanel's *The Birth of Venus*, all of which underscored the association between Venus and the sea. In poetry, a trip to Cythera was often a metaphor for (hetero)sexual intercourse. Rachilde probably knew the poem "Un voyage à Cythère" by Charles Baudelaire or, even more likely, "Cythère" by her friend Paul Verlaine in his collection *Fêtes galantes* (1869). In Alfred Delvau's *Dictionnaire érotique moderne* of 1864 (a work Rachilde would seem to have known), ref-

of naked cupids crouching beside it supported with all the strength of their fists the seashell, upholstered with blue satin. Poised on a column of Carrara marble stood Eros, his bow on his back, holding with rounded arms heavy oriental brocade curtains that fell into voluptuous folds all around the seashell, and, at the side, a bronze tripod bore an incense burner studded with precious stones where a dying pink flame gave off a vague odor of incense. The bust of the Antinous with the enameled eyes faced the tripod. The windows had been rebuilt with Gothic arches and barred like the windows of a harem, behind softly tinted stained glass windows.

The only furniture in the room was the bed. Raoule's portrait, signed by Bonnat,[58] hung surrounded by emblazoned draperies. In this canvas she wore a Louis XV hunting outfit, and a reddish greyhound was licking the handle of the whip she held in her magnificently reproduced hand.

---

erences to Venus often serve as euphemisms for sexual intercourse ("the pleasures of Venus") or related phenomena. Venereal disease was known as "a kick from Venus," and medical terminology for female genitalia included the "mountain of Venus." According to Shaw, "[A]n entry on 'common Venus' has as its definition 'the girl of the street, who only asks two francs for a voyage to Cythera'" (93).

[58]Léon Bonnat (1833–1922) was a famous French painter of portraits in a traditional, academic style.

Jacques was stretched out on the bed; with the coquetry of a courtesan expecting her lover at any minute, he had pushed away the thick blankets and the soft eiderdown. Moreover a vivifying warmth filled the snug room.

With avid eyes and passionate mouth, Raoule approached the altar of her god and in her ecstasy sighed:

"You alone exist, Beauty. I believe in you alone."

Jacques was not asleep: he sat up gently without changing his indolent pose. Against the azure background of the curtains, his supple and marvelously well-shaped torso shone as pink as the flame of the incense burner.

"Then why did you want to destroy it back then, that beauty you love?" he asked in a passionate whisper.

Raoule came and sat on the edge of the bed and seized the flesh of his slender torso in both hands.

"I was punishing an involuntary betrayal that night. Think what I would do if you ever betrayed me for real."

"Listen, dear master of my body, I forbid you to introduce suspicion between our two passions, it frightens me too much . . .

"Not on my account!" he added, laughing with his adorable childish laugh, "but on yours."

He laid his submissive head on Raoule's knees.

"It's very beautiful here," he said with a grateful look. "We're going to be very happy here."

With the tip of her index finger Raoule was caressing his regular features and tracing the harmonious curve of his eyebrows.

"Yes, we're going to be happy here, and we mustn't leave this temple for a long time, so that our love shall permeate every object, every fabric, every ornament, with its mad caresses, just as the perfume of this incense penetrates all the draperies that surround us. We'd decided to travel, but we won't go; I don't want to run away from a pitiless society whose hatred for us I feel growing more and more. We must show them that we're the stronger, since we love each other . . ." She was thinking of her aunt . . . Jacques of his sister.

"Fine," he said resolutely, "we'll stay. Besides, I'll complete my education as a serious husband; as soon as I know how to fight, I'll try to kill the wickedest of your enemies."

"I can just see it, Mme de Vénérande killing someone for me."

He fell back gracefully onto his pillow, saying:

"She has to ask to kill someone, since the means of bringing someone into the world have been absolutely denied her."

They could not help laughing out loud; and in that gaiety, both cynical and philosophical, they forgot the pitiless society that had claimed, leaving the mansion of the Vénérandes, that it was leaving a tomb.

Little by little, their insolent lightheartedness grew calmer. Its grin no longer distorted their mouths, which came together. Raoule pulled the curtain toward her, plunging the bed into a delightful semidarkness, in the heart of which Jacques's body gleamed with starlight.

"I have a capricious wish," he said, speaking only in low tones.

"It's the time for caprices," answered Raoule, putting one knee on the carpet.

"I want you to court me for real, as a bridegroom might at such a time, when he's a man of your rank."

And he wriggled, coaxingly, in Raoule's arms, which encircled his naked waist.

"So! So!" she said, pulling away. "Then I must be very proper?"

"Yes . . . See, I'm hiding, I'm a virgin . . ."

And with the quickness of a schoolgirl who has uttered a mischievous remark, Jacques gathered the sheets around him, a wave of lace fell over his forehead, and only the roundness of his shoulder could be seen. Covered thus, it looked like the wide shoulder of a woman of the people admitted by chance into the bed of a wealthy rake.

"You're cruel indeed,"[59] said Raoule, pushing the curtain aside.

"No," said Jacques, not realizing that she had begun the game already. "No, no, I'm not cruel, I'm just telling you I want to have fun . . . My heart's full of gaiety, I feel quite drunk, all loving, full of mad desires. I want to make use of my royalty, I want to make you cry out with rage and bite my wounds again as when you were tearing me apart with jealousy. I want to be ferocious in my own way too."

"Haven't I waited enough nights asking in my dreams for the pleasures that you deny me?" Raoule went on, standing up and coveting him somberly with an expression whose power had endowed humanity with yet another monster.

"Too bad," replied Jacques, sticking the tip of his moist tongue out of his purple lips. "I don't care much about your dreams; reality will be so much better afterward. I'm begging you, start right away, or I'll be angry."

"But it's the most atrocious martyrdom that you can impose on me," Raoule's trembling voice went on with

---

[59]In the French, Raoule uses the feminine form of the adjective, but since the difference in French between the masculine and feminine forms is visible but not audible (*cruel/cruelle*), Jacques does not perceive it (as the next line shows). He might, however, have picked up on the fact that Raoule used the *vous* form in this line.

its deep masculine intonation: "to wait when supreme felicity is within my grasp; to wait when you don't know how proud I am to have you in my power; to wait when I've sacrificed everything to keep you at my side night and day; to wait when the most wonderful happiness would be to hear you say: 'I'm so comfortable with my head resting on your breast, I want to sleep that way.' No, no, you can't have that much courage!"

"Yes I can," Jacques declared, genuinely put out that she did not lend herself to the comedy without having the voluptuous benefit. "I tell you it's a caprice."

Raoule fell on her knees, her hands joined, delighted at seeing him duped—so *accustomed* was he to the fraud he was begging for, not realizing that she had been using it in her passionate language for twenty minutes.

"Oh! you're so wicked! I find you completely hateful," said Jacques, irritated.

Raoule had stepped back, her head thrown back.

"Because I can't see you without going mad," she said, deceived herself in turn; "because your divine beauty makes me forget who I am and gives me a lover's thrills; because I lose my head when I see your ideal nakedness . . . And what matters the sex of these caresses to our delirious passion? What matter the proofs of attachment our bodies can exchange? What matter the remembrance of love through all the centuries and the reprobation of

182

all mortals? . . . You're a beautiful woman . . . I'm a man. I adore you, and you love me!"

Jacques finally understood that she was obeying him. He raised himself on one elbow, his eyes full of a mysterious joy.

"Come! . . . ," he said, deeply thrilled, "but don't take off that suit, since your beautiful hands suffice to chain your slave . . . Come!"

Raoule rushed to the silk bed, uncovering anew the white and supple limbs of this amorous Proteus, who now had nothing left of his virginal modesty.

For an hour this temple of modern paganism heard only long gasping sighs and the rhythmic noise of kisses, then suddenly a heartrending cry was heard, like the howling of a demon who has just been vanquished.

"Raoule," cried Jacques, his face convulsed, his teeth biting into his lips, his arms extended as if he had just been crucified in a spasm of pleasure. "Raoule, you just aren't a man! You just can't be a man!"

And the sob of lost illusions, forever dead, rose from his sides to his throat.

For Raoule had undone her white silk waistcoat and, in order to feel the beating of Jacques's heart better, she had pressed one of her naked breasts against him; a round breast, shaped like a champagne glass, with its closed flower bud that was never to blossom in the sublime pleasure of giving milk. Jacques, awakened by the brutal revolt of all his passion, pushed Raoule away from him with a clenched fist:

"No! No! Don't take that suit off," he shouted, at the height of his madness.

For once, they both played this comedy sincerely, and they had sinned against their love, which in order to live had to face the truth while fighting against it with all its strength.

Chapter 15

They had remained in the heart of Paris to fight, to brazen it out. Public opinion, that big prude, refused to engage. Everyone avoided the Vénérande mansion. Slowly Mme Silvert was crossed off the list of sought-after women; doors were not closed against her, but there were audacious ones who never crossed her threshold again. Winter functions no longer demanded her presence, and she was no longer consulted about the new play, the new novel, the novelties of fashion. They went constantly to the theater, Jacques and Raoule, but their box never opened to admit friends; they had no more friends, they were the accursed of Eden, having behind them, instead of an angel brandishing a flaming sword, an army of high-society goers. Raoule's pride held fast.

The episode of her aunt's leaving for a convent the very night of the wedding spiced up many conversations. Although no one had pitied the canoness when she was not leading the life of her dreams, she was enormously pitied now that she had at last fulfilled her dearest wish.

As for Marie Silvert, she did not reappear. In a class that had nothing to do with the society to which Raoule belonged, it was known only that a very luxurious type of establishment was being founded, and some habitués of such houses knew that a Marie Silvert would run it.

Thus it is said that the charities of saints do not always sanctify the recipients.

Nothing, however, had transpired of this in Raoule's circle; Raoule herself was unaware of this shameful fact. She was respected, that was all. And people shrank back when she passed by as they would before a woman threatened by an impending catastrophe.

One evening, with a tacit understanding, Jacques and Raoule put off the hour of pleasure. They had been married for three months, and for three months every night had found them making each other dizzy with their caresses under the blue cupola of their temple. But that evening, near a dying fire, they chatted: sometimes there is an inexplicable attraction in dying coals. Jacques and Raoule needed to chat with each other, without feminine ecstasies, without voluptuous cries, like good friends who see each other again after a long absence.

"So what's become of Raittolbe?" said Raoule, casting the smoke of a Turkish cigarette to the ceiling.

"It's true," Jacques muttered, "he's not polite."

"You know I'm not afraid of him anymore," said Raoule, laughing.

"I think it would be fun to play at being *your husband* before his bristling mustachios."

"So! Such a fatuous young man! . . ."

She added gaily:

"Shall we invite him to tea tomorrow . . . We won't go to the opera, and we won't read any old books."

"If you see nothing against it."

"A honeymoon doesn't allow any surprises, Madame," said Raoule, carrying Jacques's white hand to her lips. Jacques blushed and shrugged his shoulders with an imperceptible gesture of impatience.

The next evening the samovar was steaming in front of Raittolbe, who had offered no objection to Raoule's invitation.

The first words exchanged smacked of irony on both sides. Jacques verged on impertinence; Raoule went even further; Raittolbe emphasized it heavily.

"You've been avoiding us," said Jacques, offering him his index finger as if he were condescending.

"Can the dear baron be jealous of our happiness?" questioned Raoule, drawing herself up like an offended gentleman.

"Good heavens, my dear friend," said Raittolbe, affecting embarrassment and addressing himself only to Mme Silvert, "I always fear the manias of nervous women: if by any chance my pupil," and he indicated Jacques, "had fancied uncapping one of his foils, you know . . ."

While taking tea a few more scathing allusions were exchanged.

"You know that the Sauvarèses, the Renés, the d'Armonvilles, and even the Martin Durands avoid us," Raoule tossed out, laughing bitterly, like a devil noting his own damnation.

"They're wrong . . . I take it upon myself to replace them advantageously. One either has intimate friends or none at all," countered Raittolbe.

From that moment on, he came every Tuesday to the Vénérande mansion. The fencing lessons were taken up again in earnest; and once Jacques even went with the baron to try out a recently acquired horse. The marriage seemed to have bridged all the gulfs that had opened up before the former officer of the hussars.

He treated Jacques as an equal, and, seeing him well positioned in the saddle, a cigar in the corner of his mouth, a bold look in his eye, he thought:

"Perhaps one could yet make a man out of that clay . . . if Raoule was willing."

And he thought about a possible rehabilitation, provoked, in a moment of forgetfulness, by a real mistress, whom Raoule would have to fight with ordinary feminine tactics.

Coming back from the Bois, Jacques wished to visit Raittolbe's apartment. They pushed on to the rue d'Antin.

Jacques sniffed as he reached the interior.

"Oh!" he said, "your place reeks of tobacco!"

"Well, my sweet," Raittolbe objected mischievously, "I'm not a turncoat. I have my beliefs, and I keep them."

Suddenly Jacques cried out in surprise; he had just recognized piece by piece all the furniture from his old apartment in the boulevard Montparnasse.

"Why," he said, "I'd left them for my sister."

"Yes, she sold them on to me; not that no one else was interested, but . . ."

"What?" asked the young man, very much intrigued.

"I insisted on having them, because they're like so many chapters of a true story one doesn't wish to see published someday."

"You're very kind!" muttered Jacques, sitting down on his old oriental couch. That banal phrase was all he could find to thank the baron for his thoughtfulness. The baron sat down beside him.

"That time is far away now, isn't it, Jacques?" And he slapped him cavalierly on the thigh.

"How do you know?" muttered Jacques, leaning backward.

"What? I certainly hope that Mme Silvert will soon give us occasion to suck on some candied almonds at a christening. As for me, I want some with kirsch in them; they're the only ones I can stomach."

"Oh stop it, you bad boy!"

"Huh?" grumbled Raittolbe.

"Yes, of course, do you expect me to give birth into the bargain?"

The baron haphazardly seized a superb porcelain hookah and sent it crashing against the wall.

"Hell and damnation!" he roared. "Are you stuffed with straw? And yet I wasn't seeing things on a certain night."

"Oh, well!" said Jacques with abandon. "A bad habit is so quickly learned!"

Raittolbe paced the floor.

"Jacques," he said, "do you ever feel like trying something else without your female executioner's knowing anything about it?"

"Perhaps . . ." And Jacques smiled strangely.

"Go to your sister's at twilight, and see what's going on."

"You rake!" said Raoule's husband, shaking his pretty red head.

"You refuse?"

"No! I want some further information."

"Well!" declared Raittolbe, seized suddenly by an absurd modesty. "I'm not beating the drum for those places; but *those girls* are completely charming and knowledgeable, that's all."

"That's not enough!"

"Good God! What a lame duck!" muttered Raittolbe furiously. Jacques looked up with wondering eyes, as pure as those of a virgin, at the rough-haired rake who was speaking to him.

"What are you saying, baron! . . ."

"Well, that's funny, by God! Good heavens!"

And Raittolbe rubbed his temples; then he looked at this face, so tired yet so delicate with its features of a blond woman of pleasure.

"I can't very well tell you some story that you'll go and repeat to our wild Raoule . . . you poor excuse for a girl."

"No, I won't say anything . . . tell me anything you like . . . if it's amusing."

And, seized by an unhealthy curiosity, Jacques forgot whom he was dealing with; and almost confusing Raoule with men, and men with Raoule, he rose and leaned with both hands on Raittolbe's shoulder.

For an instant his perfumed breath brushed the baron's neck. The baron trembled to the marrow and turned away, looking at the window he would have liked to open.

"Jacques, my boy, no seduction, or I'll call the vice squad."

Jacques burst out laughing.

"A seduction in a riding jacket? Oh! what a depraved villain you are! Baron, you're being unseemly, I think! . . ."

But Jacques's laughter had become rather nervous.

"Well, I would appear less so if you were wearing a velvet coat! . . ." Raittolbe had the folly to reply.

Jacques pouted. When he saw the monster's pouting mouth, Raittolbe rushed over to the window.

"I can't breathe," he gasped.

When he came back to Jacques, the latter was shaking on the couch with irrepressible laughter.

"Go, Jacques!" he said, raising his riding whip. Then, lowering it—

"Go, Jacques!" he repeated, his voice almost failing him. "For this time you might get yourself killed."

Jacques seized his arm.

"We don't know how to fight well enough yet," he said, dragging him by force to their horses, which were prancing near the sidewalk.

They dined at the Vénérande mansion side by side, without making any allusion to the scene that afternoon that might shake Raoule's confidence.

One night, Mme Silvert entered the azure temple alone. Venus's bed remained empty, the incense burner was not lit, and Raoule did not put on her evening suit . . .

Jacques, who had gone out after lunch to see a fencing match by renowned experts, had not returned.

Toward midnight Raoule was still doubting the possibility of a betrayal. Her eyes stared mechanically at the cupid holding up the curtain; she thought she saw a mocking expression on his face.

She felt her blood freezing in her veins with unknown fright . . . She ran to the back of the room to look for a dagger hidden behind her portrait and pressed it to her breast.

She heard footsteps in the dressing room.

"It's Monsieur!" Jeanne shouted.

The maid was taking it upon herself to announce him, to reassure Madame, whose upset face had frightened her.

Indeed, Monsieur entered a few seconds later.

Raoule threw herself at him with a cry of love, but Jacques pushed her away brutally.

"What's the matter with you?" stammered Raoule, in a panic . . . "You look as though you're drunk."

"I've just come from my sister's," he said in a broken voice . . . "From my sister the prostitute . . . and not one of those girls, do you hear, not one was able to revive what you've killed, you desecrator! . . ."

He fell heavily on the nuptial bed, repeating with a grimace of disgust:

"I hate women, oh I hate them!"

Floored, Raoule retreated to the wall, and there she crumpled in a faint.

Chapter 16

"My very dear sister-in-law:

"Come this evening, about eleven, to your friend M. de Raittolbe's. You'll see some things that will please you."

"Marie Silvert."

This note was as laconic as a slap in the face. Reading it, Raoule felt a sensation of horror; however, her valiant manliness momentarily prevailed.

"No!" she cried, "he may have wanted to betray his wife . . . he's incapable of betraying his lover!"

It had been a month since Jacques had left, as it were, their sanctuary of love, and a month since, at dawn, he had asked forgiveness as a repentant *adulteress*, kissing her feet and covering her hands with tears. She had forgiven him, perhaps because at heart she was glad that he had proved to himself that he was at the mercy of her infernal power. Was it necessary that a new insult to her merciful passion should arise from the mire?

Oh! but also . . . she knew only too well, fresh and healthy flesh rules the world. She had said it so often during their maddest, most voluptuous, and most refined nights since Jacques's night of orgy. Raoule burned the note. Then the words of the note emerged in letters of fire on the walls of her drawing room. She did not want to read it again, but she saw it everywhere, from the floor to the ceiling. Raoule sent for her household retinue one by one, and asked them this question:

"Do you know which way Monsieur went tonight after his walk in the Bois?"

"Madame," answered the small groom who had held the bridle of Jacques's horse, "I think Monsieur took a cab! . . ."

This bit of information did not indicate what her husband's intentions were; yet why had he not come back to tell her about his fugue?

She was growing absolutely idiotic! . . . How could she hesitate? Isn't human nature always ready to yield to the most extravagant of temptations? Just a year ago, hadn't she herself gone to look for Jacques instead of going to look for Raittolbe?

"So," thought the wild philosopher, "he went where fate was calling him; he went where I foresaw he would go despite my demonic caresses! Raoule, the hour of reckoning has sounded for you; look danger in the face! And if it's too late, chastise the guilty."

She shuddered, because, while putting on her man's clothing so as not to be recognized on the *rue d'Antin*, she was talking aloud to herself.

"Guilty! Is he? Who knows? Must I not share the burden of a crime too often foreseen by my suspicions and to whose idea his cowardly instincts have accustomed him?"

She added, going to the service stairs that communicated with their bedroom:

"I won't chastise him! I'll be content to destroy the idol, because one can no longer worship a fallen god!" And she left, looking straight ahead, with a calm face and a crushed heart . . .

In the rue d'Antin, the concierge told her:

"M. de Raittolbe is not seeing anyone." Then, winking because he saw that this elegant young man must be an intimate friend: "There's a lady with him."

"A lady!" gasped Mme Silvert.

An atrocious supposition came immediately to mind. He might have gone to his sister first . . . At his sister's there were costumes of all sizes!

"Well, my friend, that's precisely why I want to see him! . . ."

"But it's impossible, M. the Baron is very strict about such matters."

"He gave you specific instructions! . . ."

"No . . . No need . . . you can just tell!"

Raoule went upstairs without deigning to look back and rang the bell at the door of the mezzanine. Raittolbe's personal valet answered, his finger to his mouth.

"Monsieur is not seeing anyone just now!"

"Here's my card. He has to see me!"

She had one of her husband's cards in the pocket of her coat.

"M. Silvert," stammered the bewildered servant. "But . . ."

"But," said Raoule, forcing herself to laugh, "my wife is here, I know! You're afraid that I'll make a scene? Don't worry, the police commissioner isn't following me . . ." She slipped him a banknote and closed the door behind them.

"It's true, Monsieur," murmured the poor boy, terrified, "I announced Mme Silvert hardly a quarter of an hour ago, I swear . . ."

Raoule quickly crossed the dining room and entered the smoking room, taking care to close each door she opened.

The smoking room was lit by a single candle, placed on a console. M. de Raittolbe, standing near this table, held a pistol in his hand.

Raoule made only a single bound. He too wanted to kill himself? Who had betrayed him? A beloved creature, or his moral courage? . . .

She seized the pistol, and her attack was so sudden, so unexpected, that Raittolbe let go of it; the firearm went rolling on the floor.

"You?" stammered the ex-officer, as pale as death.[60]

"Yes, you must speak before you blow out your brains, I demand it. After that . . . well! you may do as you like! . . ."

She appeared so calm that Raittolbe thought she knew nothing.

"Jacques is here!" he said in a guttural voice.

"I thought as much, since your servant announced him a short while ago."

"Dressed as a woman!" exclaimed Raittolbe, making those words into an explosion of insensate rage.

---

[60]Raoule and Raittolbe, who have been so formal with each other up to this point, now address each other in the *tu* form.

"Who would have thought!" And they looked at each other for a moment with a frightening stare.

"Where is he?"

"In my bedroom!"

"What's he doing?"

"He's crying! . . ."

"You refused!"

"I wanted to strangle him," roared Raittolbe.

"Ah! but then you wanted to blow your brains out?"

"I confess! . . ."

"The reason?"

Raittolbe could find nothing to say in response. Crushed, the rake sank down on the sofa.

"My honor is more vulnerable than yours!" he said at last.

Raoule went to the bedroom. A few minutes that seemed like centuries to the baron went by in the deepest silence.

Then a woman reappeared, dressed in a long plain black velvet dress, her head covered with a mantilla. That woman was Mme Silvert, née Raoule de Vénérande. Pale and unsteady, her husband was following her; he had put up the collar of his coat to hide the red finger marks on his neck.

"Baron," said Mme Silvert, in a steady voice, "I've been caught in flagrante delicto, but my husband doesn't want a public scandal. He will wait for you, tomorrow at six, with his witnesses, in the clearing of the woods at Vésinet."[61]

M. de Raittolbe bowed without turning to Jacques, whose head was lowered.

"Your wish is my command, Madame!" he murmured. "Except that the flagrante delicto can't be established by your husband, because Mme Silvert, I swear, isn't guilty!" And he laid his hand on his rosette of the Legion of Honor.

"I believe you, Monsieur!"

She bowed like an adversary and withdrew, her arm around Jacques's waist. Leaving the smoking room, she turned at the threshold:

"To the death!" she whispered simply in Raittolbe's ear as he was seeing her out.

The valet said later, about this strange adventure:

"Mme Silvert, whom I would have sworn as blond as wheat when she came in, was as black as soot when she went out . . . Well! In any case she is a very pretty woman!"

It was Raoule herself who came next day to rouse Jacques at dawn; she gave him the two addresses of his witnesses.

---

[61]As though to underscore the formal and ritual aspect of dueling, Raoule and Raittolbe now switch back to the *vous* form.

"Go," she said very sweetly, "and don't be frightened. It's just a matter of a fencing match in the open air, instead of in a fencing room!"

Jacques rubbed his eyes, like someone no longer aware of what he is doing; he had slept fully clothed on his satin bed.

"Raoule," he muttered with bad humor, "it's your fault! And besides, I was only joking, that's all! . . ."

"Therefore," she said, smiling with an adorable smile, "I still love you! . . ." They kissed each other.

"You'll go and do your duty as an outraged husband, you'll get a slight scratch, and that will be the only vengeance I want from you. Your opponent has been warned: he must respect your person! . . ."

"But, Raoule, suppose he doesn't obey you?" murmured Jacques, rather uneasy.

"He'll obey me!"

Raoule's tone allowed no reply.

Jacques, however, through his foggy imagination rendered stupid by vice, still saw before him Raittolbe's threatening face, and he could not understand why she, *the beloved*, forgave him in such a cowardly manner.

He found the carriage waiting near the front steps, got in mechanically, and went to the addresses indicated.

Martin Durand accepted without demur the responsibility of being a witness in an unknown affair. But Cousin

René, guessing that it had to do with some escapade of Raoule's, did not find it *amusing* to be asked to defend Jacques Silvert's honor. He yielded only when he found out that it was merely some fencing quarrel at stake.

Then, since Jacques had married a Vénérande and therefore belonged to *their nobility*, the cousin joined Martin Durand out of solidarity.

The two witnesses, not having the slightest idea what to expect, exchanged only a few words. Jacques Silvert reclined in the best padded corner of the carriage and went to sleep.

"Alexander!" said René, pointing to Raoule's husband and grinning.[62]

"Of course," answered Martin Durand, "he's fighting for the gallery. Raittolbe probably wants to make him try some new thrust. Isn't he accommodating, this husband!"

René made a haughty gesture that cut short the architect's unfortunate diatribe.

After an hour and a quarter at a fast trot by the thoroughbreds, Jacques was awakened by his witnesses and jumped down at the outskirts of the forest. It took them

---

[62]The Greek emperor Alexander was known for his ability to catnap, a factor that contributed to his military success, according to some.

a few minutes to find their adversary. Everything in this duel was unusual, and the place of rendezvous was no more clearly defined than its real motive.

Finally, Raittolbe appeared, bringing with him two former officers. Jacques knew that one salutes an opponent, and he saluted.

"He's got guts, more and more guts!" René asserted. Then the witnesses approached each other, and Jacques, to look like a real man, lit a cigarette offered by Martin Durand.

It was in the month of March, and the weather was gray but very warm. It had been raining the night before, and the new buds on the trees sparkled with a thousand shining little drops. Looking up, Jacques could not help smiling with the vague smile that for him was the entire spirituality of his soft body. What was he smiling at? Good God, he didn't know; only those drops of water had seemed to him like limpid eyes tenderly gazing down at his fate, and he felt joy in his heart!

When he saw the countryside, with Raoule on his arm, the body of that terrible creature, the master of his being, blocked out everything before him.

And he loved her very cruelly, that woman . . . It was true that he had cruelly offended her for the sake of this man who had hurt his neck so much . . .

He looked down at the earth again. Violets were poking through the grass here and there. Then, just as the raindrops had sown spangles in his darkened brain, the small dark eyes of the flowers, half veiled melancholically by the blades of grass like eyelashes, made his brain still darker.

He saw the earth surly, muddy, and he shivered at the thought of being laid there some morning, never to rise again.

Yes, indeed, he had offended this woman; but why had this man hurt his neck so much? . . .

Besides, none of it was his fault! . . . Prostitution is a disease! They had all had it in his family: his mother, his sister; how could he struggle against his own blood? . . .

They had made him *such a whore* in the most secret places of his being, that the madness of vice took on the proportions of tetanus! Moreover, what he had dared to wish for was really much more natural than what she had taught him!

He shook his red hair in the wind as he thought of these things! They were going to pose a bit with crossed swords, do some pliés. "Come along, gentlemen!"

They would cross swords till he received the promised scratch, and then he would hurry back, to make her drink in a kiss the purple pearl, no larger than the pearls of rain . . .

Yet this man had hurt his neck very much . . .

The places were marked. The choice of arms belonged to Raittolbe. He chose his own. When Jacques
took his sword from Durand's hand, he was surprised at
its weight. That displeased him: those he generally used
were very light. He took his stand in front of Raittolbe.
The "Go to, gentlemen!" spoken by one of the baron's
seconds left the adversaries together.

Jacques handled his weapon with difficulty. Decidedly,
this Raittolbe had impossible swords!

The baron didn't want to look Jacques straight in the
face, but the young man was so calm, though silent, that
Raittolbe felt his blood run cold.

"Let's get on with it," he thought, "let's rid society of
a foul creature!"

Just then the dawn tore through the gray sky. A ray of
sunshine glided up to the combatants. Jacques was illuminated, and his shirt, open to the hollow of his chest,
revealed a skin as delicate as a child's, with fine golden
hair that barely formed a shadow on his flesh.

Raittolbe feinted. Jacques parried gracefully but
rather timidly. He too was in a hurry to end it . . .
Suppose the baron made a mistake? His grip was irre-
sistible, he knew from the night before. It was the re-
ligious silence in particular that really oppressed him!
At least Raoule amused him with her biting comments

when she taught him a lesson, and he wanted to be beautiful . . .

Raittolbe hesitated a few seconds. An awful anguish gripped him, and a cold perspiration soaked his shirt.

That Jacques, all pink, seemed joyful to him! He wasn't a coward, then, that damned creature; didn't he understand that he had to defend himself? . . . So the thrusts of the sword had no more effect on his young god's limbs than the lashes from the whip.

So, not wanting to think about what was going to happen, he lunged quickly as he turned his head away a little and caught Jacques just in the middle of those red curls made lustrous by the dawn. To him it seemed as though his sword went all by itself into the flesh of a newborn babe. Jacques did not utter a cry; the unfortunate boy fell down on the tufts of grass where the dark little eyes of the violets were watching him. But Raittolbe, he did cry out; he uttered a harrowing exclamation that went to the heart of the seconds.

"I'm a wretch!" he said, in the tone of a father who has accidentally assassinated his son. "I've killed him! I've killed him!"

He rushed to the outstretched body.

"Jacques!" he begged, "look at me! Speak to me! Jacques, why did you want this, then? Didn't you know that you were condemned beforehand?[63] Oh! it's an atrocity, I can't have killed him, I love him! Say I didn't do it, sir, say it's not true. Am I dreaming? . . ."

The witnesses, distressed by this unexpected sorrow, were trying to calm him while lifting Jacques.

"For a duel to the first blood, this is a very regrettable outcome," mumbled one of the two officers.

"Yes! what a disastrous business," muttered Martin Durand.

"And there's no doctor," added René, horribly disturbed by the outcome of the adventure.

"I'm used to these things, I'll bandage him; go and fetch some water quickly . . ." said the baron's second witness.

While they were fetching some water, Raittolbe had put his lips to the wound and was trying to draw the blood that was slow in coming.

They dabbed water on Jacques's forehead with a handkerchief. He half opened his eyes.

"You're alive?" asked the baron. "Oh, my child, do you forgive me?" he went on, stammering. "You didn't know how to fight, you offered yourself to death."[64]

---

[63] All in the *tu* form.

[64] "You're alive" is said in the *tu* form, as though Raittolbe is addressing himself, but when he thinks Jacques might be able to hear him, he switches to the *vous* form.

"We confirm," interrupted one of the officers, who thought that his friend was going too far, "that M. de Raittolbe behaved perfectly."

"You must be suffering a lot, mustn't you?" the baron went on, not listening to them. "You who tremble at the least little thing. Alas! there's so little of a man in you! I must have been mad to accept this duel. My poor Jacques, answer me, I beg of you!"[65]

Silvert's eyelids opened wide; a bitter smile gripped his beautiful mouth, whose warm color was fast disappearing.

"No, sir," he stammered in a voice that had become less than a breath, "I don't hold it against you . . . it's my sister . . . who is the cause of everything . . . my sister! I loved Raoule . . . Oh! I'm cold!"

Raittolbe tried again to suck the wound, because the blood was still not coming.

Then Jacques pushed him away and said, in lower tones still:

"No, leave me, your mustache would prick me . . ."

His body shivered as he fell backward. Jacques was dead . . .

"Did you notice," said one of the baron's witnesses, when the carriage had left with the corpse, "did you

[65] Again Raittolbe uses the intimate *tu* form. Jacques replies with the *vous* form throughout.

notice that Raittolbe, in spite of his despair, forgot to shake hands with him?"

"Yes, moreover this duel was as improper as possible . . . I'm very upset about it for our friend."

On the evening of that mournful day, Mme Silvert bent over the bed in the Temple of Love and, armed with silver pincers, a velvet-covered hammer, and a silver scalpel, devoted herself to a very delicate task . . . Occasionally she wiped her tapering fingers with a lace handkerchief.

Chapter 17

The baron de Raittolbe has gone back to military service in Africa. He takes part in all the dangerous expeditions. Had he not been warned that he would die under fire?

In the Vénérande mansion, in the left wing, whose shutters are always closed, there is a walled-up room.

That room is as blue as a cloudless sky. On the bed shaped like a seashell, guarded by an Eros of marble, rests a wax figure covered with transparent rubber skin. The red hair, the blond eyelashes, the gold hair of the chest are natural; the teeth that ornament the mouth, the nails on the hands and feet were torn from a corpse. The enameled eyes have an adorable look.[66]

---

[66]Nineteenth-century culture was no stranger to morbid relics. To cite but one example, the Princess de Belgiojoso (Cristina Trivulzio),

The walled chamber has a door hidden in the draperies of the dressing room.

At night, a woman dressed in mourning, sometimes a
young man in evening clothes, opens this door.

---

a well-known fan of spiritualism in nineteenth-century France,
reputedly kept the partially embalmed body of a young man in her
wardrobe and preserved the hearts of lovers in reliquaries. Wax
figures with morbid associations were particularly commonplace in
the nineteenth century. To begin with, there were the wax models
of female figures used to teach anatomy and known as "anatomical
Venuses" (which may have suggested to Rachilde the title of her
novel—she seems to have had some knowledge of the medical
profession). These models, with detachable abdomens that revealed
the inner workings of the female reproductive system but also with
seductive poses and winsome facial features, were used as teaching
aids in the medical profession (see Showalter) and often incorporated real human body parts such as hair, just as Raoule's model
does. Waxwork displays at spectacles such as the Musée Grévin were
a popular form of entertainment, and wax models commemorated
certain historical events that resonated with cultural meaning. The
Mayerling Affair—when Rudolf (crown prince of the Hapsburg
Empire) and his mistress died in a suicide pact—did not take place
until 1889 (a date that coincides with the first French edition of
Monsieur Vénus), but it captured the popular imagination and was
marked by the preservation and reconstruction of the event through
wax figures. The prince's mistress, Marie Vetsera, was re-created,
in a wax model complete with a bleeding wound to the head, by a
Viennese collector just after the events occurred. This model later
passed into the possession of the Italian marquise Casati (Luisa
Amman, 1881–1957), a great fan of weird wax models. At one dinner
party c. 1912, one of the guests was a life-size wax statue that had
an urn containing the ashes of one of the marquise's lovers instead
of a heart. The marquise also had a wax model made of herself.
Rumor was that the model's wig was made from the marquise's own
famous red hair. The model had its own room and exact duplicates
of the marquise's designer clothes (these and other anecdotes are
reported in Ryersson and Yaccarino; see also Bloom).

209

They come to kneel beside the bed, and, after contemplating at length the marvelous lines of the wax statue, they embrace it, kiss it on the lips. A spring hidden inside the flanks connects with the mouth and animates it at the same time that it spreads apart the thighs.

This wax figure, an anatomical masterpiece, was made by a German.

Works Cited in the Notes

Apter, Emily. "Hysterical Vision: The Scopophilic Garden from Monet to Mirbeau." *Feminizing the Fetish: Psychoanalysis and Narrative Obsession in Turn-of-the-Century France.* Ed. Apter and William Pietz. Ithaca: Cornell UP, 1991. 147–75.

Baudelaire, Charles. "Du vin et du haschisch comparés comme moyens de multiplication de l'individualité." Baudelaire, *Œuvres* 243–67.

———.*Œuvres.* Vol. 1. Paris: Gallimard, 1934.

———."Les paradis artificiels." Baudelaire, *Œuvres* 269–402.

Beizer, Janet. *Ventriloquized Bodies: Narratives of Hysteria in Nineteenth-Century France.* Ithaca: Cornell UP, 1994.

Bloom, Michelle E. *Waxworks: A Cultural Obsession.* Minneapolis: U of Minnesota P, 2003.

Cheyette, Fredric L. *Ermengard of Narbonne and the World of the Troubadours.* Ithaca: Cornell UP, 2001.

DeJean, Joan. *Fictions of Sappho, 1546–1937.* Chicago: Chicago UP, 1989.

Didi-Huberman, Georges. *Invention of Hysteria: Charcot and the Photographic Iconography of the Salpêtrière.* Cambridge: MIT P, 2003.

Dumas, Alexandre, fils. *La dame aux camélias.* Paris: Livre de Poche, 1956.

Hawthorne, Melanie. *Rachilde and French Women's Authorship: From Decadence to Modernism*. Lincoln: U of Nebraska P, 2001.

Rogers, Nathalie Buchet. *Fictions du scandale: Corps féminin et réalisme romanesque au dix-neuvième siècle*. West Lafayette: Purdue UP, 1998.

Ryersson, Scot D., and Michael Orlando Yaccarino. *Infinite Variety: The Life and Legend of the Marchesa Casati*. New York: Viridian, 1999.

Schwartz, Vanessa R. *Spectacular Realities: Early Mass Culture in Fin-de-Siècle France*. Berkeley: U of California P, 1998.

Shaw, Jennifer. "The Figure of Venus: Rhetoric of the Ideal and the Salon of 1863." *Manifestations of Venus: Art and Sexuality*. Ed. Caroline Arscott and Katie Scott. Manchester: Manchester UP, 2000. 90–108.

Showalter, Elaine. *Sexual Anarchy: Gender and Culture at the Fin de Siècle*. New York: Viking, 1990.

Weil, Kari. "Purebreds and Amazons: Saying Things with Horses in Late-Nineteenth-Century France." *Differences* 11.1 (1999): 1–37.